BOUND
BY
BLOOD

THE COMPLETE SERIES

ALSO BY RICHARD FIERCE

DRAGON RIDERS OF OSNEN
Trial by Sorcery
A Bond of Flame
The Warrior's Call
The Coin of Souls
Wings of Terror
Eyes of Stone
Tooth and Claw
The Servant of Souls
Smoke and Shadow
The Dark Rider
The Song of Bones
Sword and Crown
Tides of Darkness
Wrath and Ruin
Tomb of Oaths

MARKED BY THE DRAGON
Curse of the Dragon
Scale of the Dragon
Egg of the Dragon
Call of the Dragon
Wrath of the Dragon
Sacrifice of the Dragon

THE FALLEN KING CHRONICLES
Dragonsphere
The Fallen King
The Valiant King
The Restored King

BOUND BY BLOOD

BY

BLOOD

THE COMPLETE SERIES

RICHARD FIERCE

Dragonfire Press

Print ISBN: 979-8-89631-056-3

To everyone who believed in me.

Shaoing
Shinraha Mountains
Tatenagawa
Ikje
Dangju
Zhencheng
Woncheok
Jinseong
Taepo
Kimchon
Gangcheok
Posong
Legend
Capital
Shrine
City
Mountains

RICHARD FIERCE

CHOSEN

BOUND BY BLOOD BOOK 1

CHAPTER ONE

Kai Lin was going to meet her dragon.

Chosen while she was still in the womb, she had long anticipated this moment, and also dreaded it. It should have been an exciting day, and although she was experiencing many emotions, elation was not one of them. She rubbed her sweaty palms on her gown.

"Don't fidget," Sho, her father, said softly.

"I can't help it," Kai replied.

"Leave the girl alone," her mother intervened. "She has every right to be nervous. It's an important day."

"I'm aware, Ryoko, but we haven't even entered the city yet."

Kai looked out the window of the wagon and watched the landscape pass. Her mother was right, she *was* nervous. She was leaving behind everything she had ever known for a future of uncertainty and endless war. It didn't make sense to her that both men and women were forced to be Chosen. Were it up to her, she would have taken a very different path, one less fraught with danger.

She hissed in a breath and grimaced as a lance of pain ran down the back of her skull. Clenching her jaw, she focused her attention on the swirling pattern sewn into her gown and waited for the agony to fade.

"Is it the headaches?" Ryoko asked.

Kai nodded slightly, afraid to make the pain worse.

Her mother looked at her father. "They're becoming more frequent."

"It has something to do with the ceremony," Sho answered, though Kai could tell by his tone that he was merely offering a guess.

The headaches had been rare when she was younger, but as she grew, they plagued her more and more. Now that they were headed to Ikje for the ceremony, the flashes of pain were almost like clockwork. The agony faded, and Kai unclenched her jaw.

"It seems a sorry reward for being Chosen," she said lamely.

Her parents exchanged looks, but neither one reprimanded her. Had they been in public, she knew they would have made a show of chastising her. Being Chosen was a great honor, and anyone who said otherwise was akin to a traitor.

The rest of the trip was uneventful other than Kai's steady stream of gasps when the headaches overtook her. She'd never before desired to die, but now, it was tempting to wish for the relief it offered.

The walls of Ikje came into view, and Kai marveled at the number of people who had come to attend the ceremony. Commoners and nobles alike crowded at the gates, eager to gain entry.

"We're here," her father announced.

Despite her anxiousness, Kai was curious to see the other Chosen. Were they nobles like her, or commoners? Or was there a mix? She would soon find out. The wagon trundled through a gatehouse, and guards lined the cobbled street, keeping the inquisitive at bay. That was one thing she disliked about being Chosen. She wasn't treated like everyone else. Instead, she had been kept in seclusion.

To say her childhood had been laborious was an understatement. She'd never been given dolls or other toys, had never played with another child. Upon asking about it, her parents only told her that being Chosen wasn't just an honor, it was also a sacrifice. She never understood that answer then, but she understood it now.

The wagon came to a halt, and the door swung open to reveal a soldier in leather armor. The faceplate of his helmet was missing, and his brown eyes swept over the interior, coming to rest on her. He was thin but muscular and had a stoic demeanor.

"Chosen," he greeted. "My name is Liu Wei, and I have been assigned as your personal guard. Please, follow me."

Kai stood and looked at her mother for assurance. Ryoko smiled at her, though her eyes were full of tears that threatened to spill and run down her cheeks.

"Everything will be fine," she said, rising to embrace her.

The words rang hollow in Kai's ears, but she knew her mother meant well. The lifespan of most Chosen wasn't very long, but that was to be expected when their job was to protect the kingdom from the incursion of the Drakka.

She'd had many nightmares of the terrible creatures, some so vivid she questioned if the dreams had truly been visions. The guard cleared his throat, and Kai lunged for her mother, embracing her tightly. She hugged her father next, and then she stepped out of the carriage and into an entirely new world.

Liu offered her a friendly smile and turned about, leading her across an expansive courtyard toward the castle. It towered above the city of Ikje like a sentinel, and flying overhead was a group of Sworn. Kai's breath caught in her throat at the sight of the mighty dragons soaring across the sky. Those riding upon their backs were too small to be seen clearly, but she knew they were there because their armor glinted under the sun.

Kai walked as fast as her short legs could go, but Liu was outdistancing her. He glanced back at her and slowed his pace.

"Apologies," he said. "I tend to walk fast."

Kai smiled sheepishly, but she didn't know why he was apologizing. Although she was born of a noble family, as one of the emperor's men, he likely outranked her. They reached two massive doors and at Liu's command, a host of guards scrambled to push them open.

Looking through the entrance, she saw a long hall with a vaulted ceiling. Globes of white light were spaced every six feet, and they hovered in the air of their own volition. Kai's eyes widened. She had seen magic before, but this was something much grander. She looked over her shoulder, but her parents' wagon was gone.

Her heart hammered in her chest as panic started to overtake her, but she took a deep breath and reminded herself that she would see her parents again at the Ceremony of Oaths. Kai followed Liu inside, and the doors closed behind them. She gazed around the hall. The walls were bare of any decorations, which she found odd until she realized this area was part of the barracks.

"Where are we going?" she asked.

"To your personal chambers."

"I have my own room?"

"No. All of the Chosen have been assigned to the same room, but you will each have your own bed. I expect after the ceremony you'll be transferred to Dangju for training."

"I thought we were supposed to train here?"

"Normally you would," Liu replied, turning to the right and leading her down a new hall. "We've received reports that a large force of Drakka have been seen in the area, and the general feels that it would be safest to have you train elsewhere in the event they attack the castle."

Kai frowned. The Drakka had never attacked Ikje before. Between the emperor's soldiers and the Sworn, it was too well protected. She hissed in a breath and leaned against the wall, closing her eyes against the pain of another headache.

"Are you all right?"

"I will be," she whispered in reply. After the pain subsided, she opened her eyes to see Liu staring at her, his eyes full of concern. She pushed off the wall and stumbled, but Liu caught her. He placed a hand on her forehead. His touch was surprisingly gentle, and Kai felt a rush of warmth spread through her body.

"I get headaches," she replied. "They can be rather crippling."

"We're almost there," Liu said. "Just a little further."

He supported her with his arm, and they made their way slowly down the hall, stopping at a wooden door on the right. Liu pushed it open and helped her inside. The room was spacious, with several beds lining the walls. Each bed had a trunk at its foot, and Kai assumed that was where she would store her belongings.

"You can take the last bed on the left there."

Kai looked to where Liu pointed and saw a girl that looked to be her age lying on one of the beds. She wore a chainmail shirt and had her feet crossed, her dirty boots resting on the clean, white blanket that draped the bed.

"When is the ceremony?" Kai asked, looking at Liu. Despite her curiosity about the other Chosen, she didn't really want to be left alone with them.

"In a few days. We're awaiting the arrival of the dragons. Without them, there isn't much we can do. Should I call for a physician?"

"No, I'm fine. The pain comes and goes. There is nothing that can be done for it. My parents have tried everything."

"I see. I will leave you to rest, then."

"Wait. What do we do until the dragons get here?"

"Whatever you like, so long as you remain inside the castle."

"Are we prisoners?" Kai asked.

"Of course not. It is for your protection. If you'd like to go outside, I can arrange for an armed contingent to escort you around the grounds?"

Kai hesitated. The idea of being free to do whatever she wanted was foreign to her. Finally, she shook her head.

"No, thank you. I'll stay indoors."

"Excellent," Liu said, and Kai had the feeling he was glad he wouldn't have to organize a patrol for her. "Food and water will be provided every few hours. Unless you need anything, I shall take my leave."

Although she had just met the man, she considered him a friend and was hesitant to dismiss him. She reminded herself that she had no friends, and that he was only a soldier tasked with keeping her safe.

"I do not need anything," she said.

He smiled and bowed his head to her, then left the room. Kai stood in place awkwardly for a long moment, debating on whether to lay in her bed or wander around the castle. Pain clawed at the inside of her skull, and she decided lying in bed was the better option. She walked down the row of beds, glancing at the woman in the chainmail as she passed.

The woman cracked her eyes open and returned her stare, causing Kai to look away. She climbed onto her bed and laid down, surprised at how comfortable the mattress was.

"I'm Siran," the woman said.

Kai lifted her head and looked over at her. She had her eyes closed again, but somehow it felt as though the woman was watching her.

"I'm Kai."

"You look a little soft to be a Chosen. Are you a Chosen?"

"I am."

Siran grunted. There was a long pause, and then she said, "The others were in here earlier, but they went to explore the castle. That's commoners for you. Impressed with mundane things."

"How many others are there?" Kai asked.

"Ten, I think. I didn't really count them. The servants were whispering that we're the smallest group of Chosen they've seen in years."

Kai didn't know if that was good or bad, and she didn't ask. She fidgeted with the edge of her gown, running the material under her nails. It was a nervous habit.

"You're too loud," Siran said.

"I'm sorry."

"It was a joke. Actually, you're too quiet. Say something."

"Aren't you trying to sleep?"

"No. I'm listening to my dragon."

"What do you mean?"

"He's thinking. When he thinks, I listen. It helps me learn about him."

Kai was silent for a moment, debating on whether to speak her mind. Deciding she was tired of maintaining an illusion, she spoke up.

"What's it like? Hearing your dragon, I mean?"

CHAPTER TWO

Siran sat up and looked at her. "What do you mean? You don't hear your dragon?"

"I don't think so. How would I know?"

"You would know, trust me. What *do* you hear? It should be a voice within your mind."

Kai always had a buzzing sound in her ears, and she long suspected it was related to her headaches, though whether it was the cause or a side effect, she didn't know.

"It's hard to describe, but there's a constant noise. Definitely no voice."

Siran frowned. "That's odd. I'm sure Master Satoshi will be able to help you."

"*The* Master Satoshi?"

"Yes."

Kai couldn't believe it. Master Satoshi was a hero. He'd saved the emperor's life—twice, and his list of accolades was long.

"Have you met him?"

"Not yet," Siran replied.

"Do you think the legends about him are true?"

"I'm sure there is truth to them, but like many things, they're probably exaggerated. I mean, they say he took out a dozen Drakka on his own. That's impossible."

Kai had heard that story before many times. Although she had never seen a Drakka in real life, she'd seen drawings of them. If they were anything like their illustrations, there was no way a single man could defeat an entire group of them.

"Anyway, where are you from?"

Kai hesitated before answering. She had been taught that it was unwise to reveal too much to strangers, but she decided since she'd be spending her foreseeable future with Siran and the other Chosen, it wouldn't hurt to be friends with them.

"I'm from the south. Woncheok."

"I've heard of it. Never been there, though. I'm from Posong."

"Where is that?" Kai asked.

"A week's journey southwest from Woncheok. There's nothing worth seeing there. Just farmland mostly."

"Are your parents farmers?"

Siran scoffed. "Hardly. My father is a Steward."

"So is mine."

"Thank the gods I'm not the only noble here. The others are all commoners." Siran frowned. "I don't know why they let them bond with dragons."

"It isn't up to us," Kai replied. "Dragons choose their riders."

Silence fell between them, and Kai closed her eyes. The constant buzzing sound was louder here, and the pain of another headache was coming. She tried to push it away, but it quickly overtook her.

"Are you all right?" Siran asked, noticing her discomfort.

"I will be," Kai whispered through clenched teeth.

"Do you need some water or something? Should I call for your guard?"

"No." Kai gasped in relief as the pain receded. "No, I'm fine. I get headaches sometimes."

"You should see one of the physicians about that. They can give you something for the pain."

"I've been to many of them before. Nothing helps."

"You might be surprised. I'll go with you if you want?"

Kai was caught off-guard by the woman's kindness. "I... suppose it wouldn't hurt to try."

"Follow me."

Siran led her out of the room and they traversed the hallways until they reached a large room with a high ceiling. The air was filled with the pungent scent of herbs and the low murmur of voices. Kai saw rows of beds, and some were occupied by patients in various states of health.

A gentle-faced physician sat at a wooden table, grinding dried leaves with a mortar and pestle. She looked up at Kai and smiled.

"Can I help you?"

The woman had a visage that was shaped by the passage of many years, and her white robes rustled as her wrinkled hands continued grinding away. Kai hesitated, unsure of what to say.

"She has headaches," Siran answered for her.

"Come, sit." The woman motioned to a stool beside her.

"I'll wait outside for you," Siran said. "All of this," she waved her around, "makes me uncomfortable."

Before Kai could reply, Siran turned and exited into the hall. Inhaling a deep breath, Kai walked over to the table and sat beside the woman.

"Tell me of your pain," the woman said.

"I get headaches, as she said. I've had them ever since I was young. They come on suddenly, and the pain is strong. Lately, they've gotten worse and more frequent, but every physician I've seen has been unable to help."

The woman nodded, her hands still working the mortar and pestle, but her eyes were focused on Kai. "Where do you feel the pain? Is it behind your eyes?"

"No," Kai answered. "It's near the back of my head, almost at my neck."

"I see. Lean closer. My eyes aren't as sharp as they once were."

Kai tilted her head toward the woman. She set her pestle down and placed a gentle hand on Kai's forehead. Kai felt a warm energy emanating from the physician's touch, and it soothed the faint lingering pain.

"Not all pain is of the flesh," she said cryptically.

"What do you mean?"

"There is a strange energy entwined within you."

"Are you talking about my dragon?"

"No." The woman offered no explanation. "Medicine may help you for a short time, but it will not solve your problems. You must seek the source of your pain from within and fix your *ki*. Only then will your headaches cease."

Kai blinked and furrowed her brow. The woman may as well have spoken in another language for all the sense it made.

"What do I need to do?"

"I cannot give you all the answers. I merely point you in the direction. You must do the rest."

The woman's ambiguous words were not particularly helpful, but Kai smiled anyway. Pretending was something she had grown accustomed to.

"Thank you," she said, rising from the stool.

"Take this. It will provide some relief, but only use it when the pain is unbearable. Consuming too much will dull your senses and cloud your mind."

Kai accepted a small pouch filled with herbs before returning to the hall. Siran was there waiting for her.

"Did she help you?"

"I'm not sure. She gave me this." Kai held up the pouch and Siran looked inside, wrinkling her nose.

"That stuff can be addicting. Try not to use it if you don't have to."

"That's what she told me," Kai replied.

As they walked down the corridor, the torchlight flickered against the stone walls. Kai clutched the pouch of herbs tightly, her mind replaying the physician's words.

"She said something I don't understand," Kai said, her voice echoing in the empty hallway.

"What?"

"Something about fixing my *ki*. She wasn't very clear."

"Your *ki* links you to your dragon, among other things. I don't know much beyond that. Maybe Master Satoshi will have more answers."

Kai hoped someone, anyone, would have some answers to a few of her questions. Most pressing of all, why couldn't she hear her dragon's voice if she was Chosen?

CHAPTER THREE

When they returned to their bedchamber, the other Chosen were there. A chorus of voices filled the air, all of them talking excitedly.

"What did we miss?" Siran asked loudly.

"The Sworn have captured one of the Drakka. They're securing it so we can study it safely."

Kai looked at the one who had spoken. He looked to be about the same age as her, though he was taller by roughly a foot. He had dark hair that fell messily across his forehead, and his eyes were dark and hooded. She guessed by the deepness of his tan that he worked outside, probably in the rice fields. He met her gaze, then his eyes swept her up and down.

A chill ran down her spine at the intensity of his gaze, and Kai looked away. There was something about him that made her uneasy, though she couldn't quite pinpoint what it was. He seemed normal enough.

"I'm Ichiro," he said, introducing himself. "Nice to meet you, fellow Chosen."

"I'm Kai."

"Have you seen the castle grounds yet?"

"Briefly. I've only just arrived."

"I could show you around if you'd like?"

Before Kai could respond, another of the Chosen joined them, a disarming smile parting his lips. "Don't mind him. He's just looking for an excuse to get out of training duty."

Ichiro scowled. "Ignore Jiro. He's always putting his nose where it doesn't belong."

Jiro rolled his eyes, but Kai could tell the exchange was playful. The similarity between them was apparent, and their names made it obvious they were brothers considering Ichiro meant first-born son.

As the banter between Ichiro and Jiro continued, Kai found herself relaxing in their company. The tension that had been coiled in her shoulders since she arrived at the fortress began to unwind, and she even managed a small smile at their sibling rivalry. She decided to push aside her reservations.

"Do you still want to show me the grounds?" Kai asked.

"Of course. Let's go before Jiro convinces you that he gives better tours," Ichiro joked, earning a playful shove from his brother.

Kai looked at Siran, who remained standing quietly at her side. "Do you want to come with us?"

She thought the girl would decline, and was surprised when Siran shrugged.

"Sure."

The group set off through the labyrinthine corridors of the castle, passing bustling servants and nobles going about their business. Ichiro proved to be a knowledgeable guide, regaling Kai with tales of the fortress's history and pointing out hidden nooks and crannies where one could escape for a moment of solitude.

As they strolled through an open garden filled with fragrant blooming flowers, Kai noticed a figure standing at the edge of the garden, watching them with intense interest. The person was cloaked in shadow, their features obscured. Kai's breath caught in her throat, sensing a strange familiarity emanating from the mysterious figure. Before she could react, the person turned and disappeared into the shadows, leaving Kai feeling a sense of unease prickling at her skin.

"Did you see that?" Kai whispered to Siran, who shook her head.

"See what?" Ichiro asked, glancing around.

"Nothing. Never mind."

Ichiro continued the tour, but Kai couldn't shake off the feeling of being watched. She noticed fleeting glimpses of movement in the corners of her vision and heard whispers carried by the wind that seemed to speak her name. Each time she turned to investigate, there was nothing there.

They reached a secluded part of the garden, and Ichiro stopped and turned to Kai, a mischievous glint in his eyes. "There's a hidden passage here that leads to a lookout point with a stunning view of the valley. Care to see it?"

Kai hesitated. Despite knowing they weren't supposed to venture outside the castle, she felt the allure of rebelliousness. She'd spent her entire life living under the rule of law... what was one transgression? Besides, once she was Sworn, she may not live long enough to enjoy another moment like this. She nodded.

Ichiro led the way, and they filed into a narrow passage concealed by overgrown vines and moss-covered stones. The air grew cooler as they descended underground, the faint sound of dripping water echoing around them. The path sloped upward, and they emerged on the other side of the wall.

The dense canopy above cast dappled shadows on the ground, and Kai's unease heightened. The air seemed to grow heavier with each step they took. Ichiro continued guiding them, his steps sure and confident. The trees opened up to a clearing where a stone plateau overlooked the valley below. Ichiro walked to the edge of the plateau and gestured grandly towards the sprawling valley below.

"Behold, the lands we will protect once we are Sworn," he proclaimed.

As the rest of them stepped onto the plateau, a sudden gust of wind whipped through the clearing, causing the trees to sway and creak. Kai shivered, feeling a sense of foreboding creep over her. The view of the valley lay before them, and the sky was bathed in hues of orange and red by the setting sun. Kai stepped closer to the edge, her heart pounding in her chest as she took in the breathtaking scenery.

In the distance, she noticed something peculiar on the horizon. A dark cloud was rapidly approaching, billowing and churning in an unnatural manner. Fear prickled at the back of her neck, and she turned to the others with wide eyes.

"What is that?" she asked.

Ichiro's confident demeanor faltered for a moment as he followed Kai's gaze to the ominous cloud. His expression turned grim, his jaw clenching.

"It looks like a storm," he replied.

Jiro took a step back, his playfulness replaced with nervousness. "We should go back. Now."

Ichiro nodded, not bothering to argue. They retreated back through the damp, dark tunnel and a sense of urgency hung in the air. Kai's mind swirled with thoughts of the approaching storm. What kind of storm moved with such malevolence and speed? And why did it fill her with a primal fear she couldn't shake?

Emerging back into the garden, they were met with an eerie stillness that contrasted sharply with the chaos looming on the horizon. The once vibrant colors of dusk had faded into a somber palette as dark clouds gathered overhead, blotting out the last remnants of sunlight. A peal from the bell tower broke the stillness, a deep resonant tone that reverberated throughout the castle grounds.

"Let's get inside," Siran said, her tone full of authority.

Ichiro and Jiro sprinted off. It was obvious they were used to taking orders. Kai glanced up as rain began to patter around them, and she hurried to catch up to Siran. They entered the main hall and Kai noticed a hush had fallen over the fortress.

The servants moved with a practiced silence, their footsteps barely audible as they went about their duties. The nobles mingled and conversed in hushed tones, their words carrying an air secrecy. A group of Sworn passed by, their tense expressions hinting at the weight of their responsibilities.

"What's happening?" Kai whispered.

"I don't know… but we should probably be prepared for the worst."

CHAPTER FOUR

The strange storm laid siege to Ikje for two full days. The howling wind and relentless rain battered the fortress, causing water to seep through cracks and leak into the library. Kai and the other Chosen were forced to help the servants, who scrambled madly to staunch the flow. They mopped the floor and moved valuable tomes to safer areas.

The landscape outside the fortress fared worse. Ancient trees that had withstood all manner of ill weather burst into flames from lightning strikes, reduced to ruins in an instant. Rivers swelled and overflowed their banks, washing away shoots of grain that already struggled to grow.

When she wasn't helping the servants, Kai spent her time looking out the window. The ominous darkness that shrouded Ikje seemed to seep into her very bones, filling her with a deep sense of foreboding. As the hours stretched into days, whispers began to circulate among the castle that a curse had befallen Ikje, that a vengeful spirit was unleashed for some unknown transgression. Kai tried to dismiss these rumors as mere superstition, but she couldn't shake off the feeling of being watched, of unseen eyes following her every move.

On the morning of the third day, the storm abated. Kai awoke to someone pounding loudly on the door to their chamber. She sat up and looked around groggily. The other Chosen were slower to move. They were as exhausted as she was, and she didn't blame them for not wanting to stir. The door swung open, and Liu strode into the room, followed by a dozen other guards.

"Rise and prepare yourselves," Liu said. "Breakfast is ready in the dining hall, and once you have eaten, you will come to the dungeon to study the Drakka."

Kai's stomach turned at the thought of seeing one of the creatures in the flesh. The guards left, and the Chosen hurriedly dressed and made their way to the dining hall, where a simple meal of rice and bread awaited them. Kai ate in silence, her thoughts weighing heavily on her. She wondered how her parents had fared during the storm. No one had brought word that anything had happened to them, so she assumed they were well.

After their meal, Liu and the other guards led them to the dungeon. Torches flickered along the stone walls, and the air was musty and warm. The sound of dripping water echoed in the shadows, remnants from the storm.

The dungeon was a series of winding tunnels lined with prison cells. They continued onward until they reached a dead-end where a heavy iron door blocked the way ahead. Liu produced a set of keys and unlocked the door, then motioned for them to enter. Kai exchanged looks with the other Chosen before stepping across the threshold.

The room was well illuminated with spheres of white light that bobbed overhead. Several figures in blue robes trimmed in gold lined the walls, their complete focus on the hulking form in the center of the chamber. Chained to the stone floor was a creature unlike anything Kai had ever seen before.

It possessed a muscular frame with broad shoulders, and its skin was a green hue that glistened like wet clay. A mane of wild, jet-black hair cascaded down its back in tangled waves. The creature's visage was a grotesque mask of fury and malice. Two long, curved horns protruded from its head, sharp and gleaming like polished ebony. Smaller horns arced back from its shoulders, and its nose was broad and flat, nostrils flaring with each exhalation, while a wide mouth revealed rows of sharp, yellowed fangs that seemed designed to rend flesh from bone.

Adorning its powerful limbs were iron-studded bracers and anklets. Clawed hands, each digit tipped with talons as black as night, looked capable of crushing stone and tearing through armor with ease. Hanging loosely from its hips was a tattered loincloth, the only semblance of clothing it wore.

Kai felt her breath catch as she took in the sight. She had heard tales of the Drakka since she was a child—of their fearsome power and insatiable hunger for destruction. To be standing so close to one now sent a wave of dread down her spine.

Liu stepped forward, his voice steady but laced with caution. "This is our enemy. They are dumb creatures, but what they lack in wits they make up for in brute strength and viciousness. Note its green skin. Can any of you tell me what that signifies?"

"I can," Siran answered. "Green Drakka have power over the earth."

"Someone has spent some time studying," Liu said, sweeping his gaze over others. "Green are the most common, but there are others. For now, we will focus on this one. Drakka are strong beyond measure, but they are not invincible. Your dragon can easily dispatch one, but if you find yourself battling one alone, your best option is to strike here." Liu stepped closer to the beast and motioned to its chest. "A sharp blade to the heart will be sufficient."

The Drakka strained against the chains, and despite Liu's confident manner, he jumped back. The chains held, and the Chosen chuckled nervously.

"We have him bound," one of the robed men said. "He will not break free."

Kai turned her attention to the man. His blue robes indicated he was an Inquisitor, a soldier of the empire gifted with the power to control magic. Kai had never met an Inquisitor, but he seemed an ordinary man like any other.

Liu continued his lesson, pointing out the various weak points on the Drakka's body and how to defend against its brutal attacks. The Drakka shifted its weight, muscles rippling beneath its emerald skin. It seemed to radiate a primal energy that both intrigued and terrified Kai. She couldn't tear her gaze away from the creature, despite the unease churning in her stomach. The beast flicked its gaze back and forth from Liu to the Inquisitors. He'd said they were dumb, but Kai sensed the Drakka was studying them, calculating a way to escape.

"You all look terrified," Liu said, bringing Kai's attention back to him. "As well you should be, but soon you will no longer be Chosen. You will be Sworn, and as such, it is your duty to protect and defend the empire from them. Kai, come closer."

Kai's spine stiffened at the mention of her name. She met Liu's gaze, and he nodded slightly. He was tasked with protecting her, so if he didn't think there was any chance of the Drakka harming her, then she should trust him... shouldn't she? She swallowed hard and slowly drew closer to the creature.

It ignored her at first, but its nostrils flared, and it whipped its head toward her.

"Calm your fears," Liu instructed. "Match its gaze and let it know you are not afraid."

Kai looked up at the Drakka and met its stare. Her knees trembled, but she kept her face from contorting in fear. The creature sniffed the air once, twice, and then it leaned down, regarding her curiously. There was an intelligence in its eyes. She could see it clearly. Something inside her willed her to reach out her hand.

Hesitantly, she lifted her right hand and stretched it forth. The Drakka sniffed again, then its eyes hardened, the intelligence replaced by fury, and it snarled and tried to snap its jaws onto her flesh. Her feet tangled up as she tried to move, and she fell hard on her backside, her eyes wide with terror. The Drakka flexed its massive muscles, stretching the chains taut. A flash of blue light illuminated the chamber, temporarily blinding her. The Drakka shrieked in pain and anger.

Kai blinked rapidly until her vision cleared. Liu stood over her and offered his hand. She grabbed it, and he pulled her onto her feet.

"What were you doing?" he asked quietly, shifting his eyes from her to the other Chosen.

"I... I don't know."

"Never do that again."

Kai nodded. Her throat constricted, and swallowing didn't help. She retreated back to where the other Chosen stood and stared at the Drakka. There was something... familiar about the creature. She knew that was impossible, and yet she'd felt it. An intangible sensation deep down in her being.

What could it mean?

CHAPTER FIVE

The rest of their time with the Drakka was uneventful. Kai wanted to clear her mind, and Siran didn't feel like joining her, and so Liu followed her at a distance as she wandered the garden. The cobblestones were still slick from the rain, but the sun was high overhead and here and there she spotted sections of the pathway that were drying.

She couldn't get the sight of the Drakka from her mind. Glancing over her shoulder at Liu, she nodded for him to join her.

"Is everything all right?"

"Yes," she replied. "How much longer before the dragons arrive for the ceremony?"

"They should arrive within the next day or two. The storm delayed their arrival. While it isn't ideal, the servants are glad. It gives them more time to prepare for the ceremony. Everything was ruined from the rain."

One person's misfortune is another's blessing, she thought to herself. She closed her eyes as a wave of pain washed over her, but it quickly faded. The headaches had lessened over the past few days, and she hadn't needed to take any of the medicine the healer had given her.

"I want to ask you something."

"Speak your mind."

"I fear you will think I am crazy," Kai admitted.

"Fear should not stop you from seeking answers."

"How easily you say that." She stared at some flowers, trying to figure out how to phrase her question. "You said Drakka are not intelligent, but how do we know that?"

"We have studied them long enough to make that judgement based on their behavior. There are countless reasons why we believe this to be true. They are driven only by instinct. There are no leaders among their ranks. They consume everything without thought or concern for even their own continuation."

"Then why haven't we defeated them?"

Liu laughed, but there was nothing humorous about her question. "You are not the first to ask that, but I do not have an answer. Despite how many we kill, their numbers never seem to decrease."

Kai frowned, troubled by his words. She couldn't rid herself of the feeling that there was more to the Drakka than met the eye, that there was a depth to them that had yet to be understood. A gust of wind blew through the garden, and the scent of damp earth reminded her of home.

"Are my parents well? From the storm, I mean."

"They are fine. I confirmed so myself after the storm passed."

"That is good. Thank you for checking on them."

As they strolled along a path lined with vibrant camellia, Kai gathered her courage to voice her true question. "What if we've been wrong about the Drakka all this time?"

"How so?"

"What if they're smarter than we realize? Perhaps they've only led us to believe they lack intelligence."

"The notion that the Drakka could possess a level of intelligence we have yet to comprehend is unsettling, to say the least. But the empire's best minds have studied them extensively. Even if they are smarter than we know, we have strategies in place to protect ourselves."

"But what if our strategies are based on faulty assumptions?" Kai pressed on, her mind racing with the implications of her own words. "What if we need to rethink everything we know about the Drakka in order to truly defeat them?"

Liu regarded her thoughtfully. "I must admit that your questions give me pause, but not because I think you are crazy," he added, silencing her before she could protest. "Your line of thinking challenges everything we know, so it is difficult because... I do not have the answers. Let us assume you are correct about this. What then shall we do?"

Kai stared at him, speechless. What indeed? "Like you, I do not have an answer. Earlier..." she trailed off, uncertain if she should say anything.

"Earlier...?"

"I had the feeling *it* was familiar to me somehow."

"Have you encountered this one before?"

"No. Until today, I've never seen a Drakka. I know it doesn't make sense, but I *felt* it."

"I still do not think you are crazy, but I am concerned about this. I will speak with Master Satoshi. Perhaps he can give us guidance. Did your dragon also feel it?"

Kai's eyes darted away from Liu. She couldn't tell him the truth. If the news broke that a Chosen could not hear the voice of their dragon, there was no telling what the response would be. People might accuse her mother of lying about feeling the Sign. She imagined it would result in dishonor.

"I've not consulted my dragon about this," Kai answered. It wasn't a lie, not really.

"I would suggest you do so. If your dragon felt it... well, we would need to investigate this further."

Kai nodded.

"In the meantime, do not speak of this to anyone else." Liu cleared his throat and changed the subject. "The ceremony is almost upon us. I imagine you are excited to meet your dragon face to face?"

"If I am honest, I am nervous. Being Chosen is a great honor, but I do not feel worthy."

"If you were not, your dragon would not have selected you. Still, I understand in my own way. I do not feel worthy of protecting a Chosen."

"Why not?"

Liu smiled. "You do not want to know of my faults."

"We are all flawed. You know that I am nervous and afraid. Tell me why you think you are not worthy."

"Your life is in my hands," he replied. "I am not confident that I am capable of ensuring your safety. It is an immense burden."

"I know I've only been here for a few days, but there doesn't seem to be any danger here. I think things will be fine. Besides, once I am Sworn, you will no longer be assigned to me."

A horn sounded in the distance. Kai startled, her heart leaping in her chest. Liu turned his attention west.

"They're early," he said.

"Who?"

"The dragons."

CHAPTER SIX

The courtyard was a cacophony of voices as people gathered to watch the arrival of the dragons. Liu and Kai stood among the crowd, starting westward. The silhouettes of a dozen dragons appeared on the horizon, their majestic forms cutting through the sky with grace and power.

The people around her gasped and whispered in awe. Kai held her breath as she watched the dragons draw nearer, their scales shimmering in the sunlight. Each dragon was unique, with vibrant colors and patterns that set them apart from one another. Emerald, sapphire, amethyst and other colors greeted them, but Kai's attention was drawn to one dragon in particular. Its scales glistened like polished gray hematite, and Kai had no doubt that was her dragon.

The buzzing in Kai's ears intensified, building to a crescendo and drowning out the sounds of the crowd around her. Thankfully, there was no pain, but that didn't make her feel any better. The dragons landed in the field outside of the castle, each one issuing a thunderous roar which she faintly heard. The noise was overwhelming, and she felt her legs grow weak. Fearing she was about to pass out, she grabbed hold of Liu's arm. The buzzing abruptly stopped.

"Another headache?" he asked lowly.

Kai offered a brief nod, not wanting to add to his concerns. "It passed quickly," she replied.

A cheer erupted from the crowd as a figure strode across the ramparts of the wall. He raised his right hand, calling for silence.

"Good people of Ikje, thank you for coming to honor our Chosen. This group is only a dozen strong, but as we all know, the strength of a rider is worth many. Tonight, we will celebrate our Chosen with a feast, and tomorrow, they will be Sworn!"

The crowd bellowed their approval, and the man on the parapet returned to the castle.

"Who was that?" Kai asked.

"That was Master Satoshi."

As the sun began to set, lanterns and braziers were lit around the courtyard, bathing everything in a warm light. Long tables were arranged in the courtyard, laden with an abundance of food and drink, and soon, the courtyard was alive with laughter and chatter as people mingled, celebrating the upcoming ceremony. Kai sat between Siran and Ichiro, swept up in the festivities, her earlier doubts and worries momentarily pushed aside by the joyous atmosphere. She ate and drank with the others, listening to stories of past ceremonies and legendary deeds of riders from their history.

As the night progressed, the crowd slowly dispersed and a chill settled in the air. Kai excused herself from the table and slipped away into the shadows of the courtyard, making her way through the maze-like corridors of the castle. She found a secluded alcove overlooking the moonlit landscape beyond the walls and leaned against the cool stone, wrapping her arms around herself as a shiver ran down her spine.

The moon was full and bright, casting a silvery glow over the landscape. From this vantage point, she could see the dragons resting in the field beyond the walls, their forms barely visible in the darkness.

"Kai?"

She started at the sound of her name and turned to see Liu, his expression unreadable.

"Are you all right?"

"Yes. Just... thinking."

"Master Satoshi has requested your presence."

"Is it about what I told you?"

He nodded in reply. Kai was exhausted and wanted nothing more than to crawl into her bed, but she knew Master Satoshi's request was an order, not an invitation. She pushed off the wall and Liu escorted her through the hall.

"What did he say when you told him?"

"Not much. He listened, and then asked to see you. I suppose he wants more details."

Kai followed Liu in silence. They climbed a circular staircase to the highest tower of the castle and paused outside a set of oak doors. Liu gave a firm knock, announcing their presence, and they were bid to enter.

Kai entered the room first. Master Satoshi sat at a large wooden desk cluttered with scrolls and other parchments. He looked up and motioned for her to take a seat. The room was brightly lit by a myriad of lanterns. She walked to his desk and sat down, folding her hands in her lap.

Master Satoshi's face was chiseled with sharp, angular features—high cheekbones, a strong jawline, and a straight, narrow nose that looked as though it could have been sculpted from stone. Dark, penetrating eyes reflected the calm of a seasoned warrior, and his jet-black hair was tied back in a soldier's knot. He exuded a quiet confidence, his presence commanding respect and attention. Awestruck, Kai stared at him in silence. The man was a hero, a paragon of strength and honor.

"Liu tells me you felt a connection to the Drakka. I would like to hear you recount the experience in your own words."

"Yes, my lord." Kai ran her fingers along the material of her clothes, looking for a seam to run under her nails, but there wasn't one. "It was earlier, when we were studying the creature. Liu had asked me to come closer to it, and when it looked at me..."

"Go on."

"I felt something. It's hard to describe, but it was as though I knew this creature."

"Liu said you've never seen a Drakka before today. Is that correct?"

"Yes, my lord."

Satoshi's eyebrows furrowed in thought. "And what has your dragon said about this matter?"

"I have not spoken to it yet."

Satoshi's eyes moved from her to Liu, who was standing at attention near the door. "Leave us," he instructed. Liu did as commanded and closed the door behind him.

"Is there anything else you want me to know?"

"Not that I can think of," Kai replied.

Satoshi sat back in his chair and stared at her, his gaze holding the intensity of an unyielding tempest. "Trust is a two-way path, Kai Lin. How can I trust you if you lie to my face?"

Kai's cheeks flushed with warmth. "I-I'm sorry, my lord." Her hands trembled as she fidgeted. Satoshi's expression softened slightly as he observed her distress.

"Honesty is paramount in our order. We rely on trust and transparency to uphold our values and traditions," he explained with a measured tone. "Now, let us try this again. Is there anything else you want me to know?"

Kai's eyes watered with tears, and despite her best efforts to hold them in, one slipped free and slid down her cheek. She opened her mouth to speak, closed it, and clenched her fists. What she was about to say could bring disaster upon her family.

"I have never spoken to my dragon."

CHAPTER SEVEN

"I suspected as much."

Kai waited for the confusion, the outrage, the repercussions that would surely follow. Instead, Master Satoshi remained eerily calm, his gaze unwavering. Kai's heart pounded in her chest, unsure of what would come next.

"Why have you not spoken to your dragon?"

"I… I cannot hear it. There is only a buzzing sound in my mind. I've tried countless times to communicate with it, but it is no use. I fear I am not truly Chosen."

"Silence does not mean absence. It could be that your dragon is waiting for you to listen in a different way."

Confusion clouded Kai's mind. What did he mean by a different way? She had been trying to communicate with her dragon through thoughts and feelings as she had been taught, but to no avail.

"I have tried everything I can think of," she said.

"You need not fear judgment here. I am not quick to condemn, especially in matters concerning the bond. It is a sacred connection, one that cannot be forced or coerced. For some, the bond is tentative, weak. It is like a muscle. It needs to be used, exercised. You are not the first Chosen to have this problem, though it is not common."

Kai felt a weight lift off her shoulders at his words. She met his gaze, seeing understanding and empathy reflected in his eyes. "I was afraid..."

"You were afraid of being misunderstood," he finished for her. "But I assure you, I have seen many riders face similar struggles when it comes to communicating with their dragons. It is a process that takes time and patience. For many, it is merely a matter of meeting their dragon. Seeing them in the flesh can help solidify the bond."

Kai absorbed Master Satoshi's words, feeling a glimmer of hope ignite within her. His words eased the fears that had plagued her for so long. Perhaps he was right. She nodded slowly, grateful for his understanding and guidance. The words of the healer suddenly came to her.

"Someone told me I had a strange energy in my *ki*. Do you know what she meant?"

"*Ki* is the life force that flows within us, connecting us to all things in the world. It is said that each individual's *ki* is unique, a reflection of their essence and spirit. I am no healer, but I would wager a guess that the shame you feel has muddied your *ki*. Cleanse it, and it may help to unlock your connection to your dragon."

"How would I do that? Even with your explanation, I'm not entirely sure what my *ki* is."

"The easiest way is to meditate. Visualize your *ki* and filter out the negative energy that taints it. The process is time consuming, but I believe you will find it well worth the effort."

"Thank you, my lord. You have lifted a great burden from me."

"I only do what I would expect anyone else to do for me. Go and get some rest. The ceremony is tomorrow, and you will need a clear mind."

Kai rose from her chair and offered a bow to Satoshi. He hid his smile by yawning and waved her away. When she reached the door, he told her to inform Liu he was dismissed for the evening. She nodded and stepped into the hall. Liu was leaning against the wall, his arms folded across his chest and his eyes half lidded. At the sound of the creaking door, he straightened.

"He said you are dismissed, which appears to be a good thing since you were dozing off just now."

"I was merely resting my eyes," Liu replied.

A faint smile graced Kai's lips, the first genuine one she had shown in quite some time.

"How did it go?"

"Much better than I expected," she said. "Master Satoshi is as gracious as he is wise."

"Good. What did he say about your Drakka experience?"

"Nothing. I think he's as baffled about it as I am."

"Why did he keep you so long?"

"We talked about other things," Kai replied evasively. "He suggested I cleanse my *ki*."

Liu grunted in response. They returned to the main floor of the castle, and Liu walked with her until they reached the door to her room.

"Get some sleep," he said as he departed. "Tomorrow will be a long day."

Kai opened the door and slipped inside. The other Chosen were in bed, and judging by the chorus of snores and heavy breathing, they were all sleeping. She quietly crept to her bed and stripped down to her undergarments, then laid down and stared up at the shadows that shrouded the ceiling. For the first time in years, she felt at peace.

Satoshi's words echoed in her mind, urging her to cleanse her *ki* to make way for a stronger connection with her dragon. Closing her eyes, Kai focused on her breathing. She delved deep into herself, visualizing her *ki* as a bright orb within her core. Surrounding it was a murky haze that dulled its radiance.

With each breath, she imagined the light growing stronger, pushing back against the darkness that sought to dim it. The weight of shame and self-doubt began to lift as she focused on letting go of the negative energy that had clouded her spirit. It was a slow process, requiring patience and fortitude, but Kai was determined to forge a deeper connection with her dragon.

The haze dissipated, and a faint whisper tickled at the edges of her consciousness. It was not a sound she heard with her ears but a sensation that resonated within her being. Intrigued, Kai opened herself to it, inviting the whisper into herself.

Images flickered in her mind's eye—vivid flashes of scales, an endless expanse of azure sky, and the sensation of soaring through clouds. The whisper grew stronger, manifesting as a gentle warmth spreading from her core. In that moment of surrender, Kai felt a presence, a gentle touch brushing against her spirit.

The buzzing she had always heard began to shift, morphing into a symphony of harmonious vibrations that resonated deep within her soul. It was a feeling that transcended words. Like a gentle breeze stirring dormant embers, she felt a presence rousing within her. It was as if a part of herself she had long neglected was awakening, stretching its wings in the darkness of her inner self. The connection she had yearned for but thought unattainable was now tangible, a thread linking her to a being of immense power and ancient wisdom.

Tears pricked at the corners of Kai's eyes as she reveled in the newfound connection. It was as if a missing piece of her soul had finally been found, completing a puzzle she hadn't even known was incomplete.

Exhaustion overtook her, and as she drifted off to sleep, she was comforted by the knowledge that she was no longer alone.

CHAPTER EIGHT

When Kai opened her eyes, the warm light of the morning sun streamed in through the window. She sat up and stretched, a newfound energy coursing through her body. For the first time in her life, she was eager to meet her dragon in person.

She reached out with her thoughts, but although she sensed the same strong presence from the previous night, she still couldn't hear her dragon's voice. Satoshi's words lingered in her mind, and she was confident that today would be the day she finally heard her dragon speak.

Kai climbed out of bed and noticed a pile of clothes folded neatly atop the chest at the end of her bed. A pair of black leather boots sat beside the clothes, and they shined with fresh polish.

"They expect us to look nice," Siran said. "The Ceremony of Oaths is sacred, so on and so forth." Kai looked at her. She was fully dressed in the same clothes but was lying in her bed, propped up on her elbows. Suddenly feeling immodest, she hurriedly dressed herself.

"You don't think it's important?"

"Of course I do, but after we are trained, they throw us against the Drakka. Who cares what we wear to the ceremony? No one is going to remember that. What they remember is how we die."

"That's a little depressing, don't you think?"

"It is, but that doesn't make it any less true. Besides, it's not like anyone will be able to see these under the armor."

Siran's dark words couldn't bring her spirits down. The joy inside her was too strong to be quenched.

"That's fair," Kai replied. She'd almost forgotten that she'd been fitted for armor before leaving home. She ran her hands along the bright red material of her new clothes, admiring the softness.

"Silk," Siran said, as if reading her thoughts.

Kai nodded, impressed by the fine quality of the fabric. It felt like a caress against her skin, a feeling she wasn't accustomed to. As she finished putting her boots on, the door creaked open, and Liu entered the room with the other guards. His expression softened as he took in Kai's appearance.

"You look nice," he said, a hint of pride in his voice.

Kai felt her cheeks warm at the unexpected compliment. "Thank you."

"We've got several things to do before the ceremony, so we should get to it."

"Can we eat first? I'm hungry."

"Breakfast is being served now. Just be sure not to get your clothes dirty."

Kai and the other Chosen went to the dining hall and ate a quick meal, then they were ushered to the armory. Inside, the air was thick with the scent of metal and leather. Rows of weapons lined the walls, each gleaming under the warm glow of oil lamps. Kai marveled at the craftsmanship on display, from the intricate engravings that adorned the blades of swords to the finely woven strings that dangled from their hilts.

A white-haired smith approached them, his weathered face breaking into a toothy grin. "Honored Chosen," he greeted, gesturing for them to follow him to a row of armor stands, each holding a set of gleaming armor.

"Let's start with you," he said, pointing at Jiro.

"Lucky," Ichiro muttered, playfully punching his brother in the arm.

Jiro stepped forward and the smith took a few measurements, then motioned to one of the stands. "This one is yours." Kai watched as the smith aided with putting the individual pieces on, adjusting straps and buckles with practiced ease. Jiro stood tall in his new armor, the metal plates clinking together as he moved. Next, it was Ichiro's turn. Despite his playful demeanor, Kai could sense there was a fire within him that burned fiercely. Commoner or not, something told her that he would be a great warrior.

Once Ichiro was suited up, it was Siran's turn. She stood confidently as the smith worked around her, his hands deftly securing each piece in place. Siran looked every bit the warrior, and Kai was glad to count her as a friend.

Finally, it was Kai's turn. She stepped forward eagerly, her heart pounding in anticipation. The smith measured her, then pointed at the stand that held her armor. As he helped her don the pieces, Kai felt a sense of belonging wash over her. The weight of the armor was comforting rather than burdensome, and it fit her perfectly.

Once fully armored, Kai took a few experimental steps, testing the flexibility. Surprisingly, she found it easier to move in than she had anticipated, the armor fitting her like a second skin. She flexed her fingers within the cotton gloves and smiled in admiration.

After each of them had been outfitted, the white-haired smith nodded in approval, a glint of pride in his eyes. "You all wear it well," he said. "It is an honor to have crafted your armor. Now, you must choose a weapon."

The room was filled with an array of options, all of them deadly. The Chosen spread out, and Kai walked over to a rack of swords. Her hands ghosted over the polished handles of a few, but nothing caught her eye. She continued to the far wall and her eyes fell upon a sword unlike any other in the room.

The blade was as dark as the void and sharp enough to split a hair. Its edge, honed to perfection, caught the light in razor-thin, iridescent lines that seemed to dance before her eyes. The surface, smooth as a still lake at midnight, bore intricate runes that emanated magical power. The hilt was wrought from lustrous ebony and wrapped in dark leather. The crossguard flared out like the wings of a raven, its tips fashioned into menacing, curved talons, providing balance and protection. Nestled in the pommel was a perfect, unblemished obsidian, its surface as dark and reflective as a night sky without stars.

Kai reached out and wrapped her fingers around the hilt, pulling it off the wall prongs. Something clattered to the floor, and she whirled around in surprise. The smith's eyes were wide, and he dropped to his knees and pressed his forehead to the floor. Kai looked at Liu, who was staring at her in a similar fashion.

"I'm sorry," she said. "Should I not have touched it? I'll return it."

She turned to put the sword back, but the smith's words stopped her.

"That blade has not been touched since its creation. It was forged from volcanic rock, and the smith who crafted it weaved a spell into the metal. Only one baptized in the blood of dragons can wield it."

Kai's eyes roamed the length of the blade, then she looked at the smith, her brows scrunched in confusion. "I have never seen a dragon, let alone touched the blood of one."

The smith and Liu engaged in a whispered conversation, then Liu rushed out of the room, leaving Kai further bewildered. The smith approached her slowly, almost reverently.

"Whether you know it or not, you must have come in contact with dragon blood. There is no way you would be able to touch the sword otherwise. Unless..."

"Unless what?" she asked.

"Unless the spell has faded. I am too old now to risk the pain it would cause." The smith turned to the other Chosen. "Would one of you be willing to try holding the sword?"

They stared at Kai as though she were some sort of apparition, all except Siran. The woman confidently strode over and extended her right hand. Kai offered her the weapon, and as soon as Siran touched it, a dazzling burst of energy shocked her. Siran cried out and staggered back, pressing her hand to her chest.

"I am sorry, but I needed to be sure," the smith said. "Go and see the healers. They will tend to your hand and ensure you are fit for the ceremony."

Siran departed, and Kai couldn't help but feel a twinge of guilt even though it wasn't her fault. "I do not want this sword," she said softly.

"It was made for you," the smith insisted. "What happened to her has happened to all who have tried to touch that blade. The fact you hold it now and are not immobilized with pain confirms you are its owner now."

His words weighed heavily on her as she gazed at the weapon, torn between the allure of the weapon and the danger it seemed to pose. She stilled her racing heart and reached out to her dragon. Again, she did not hear a voice, but something told her she should keep it. After a moment of contemplation, she nodded.

"I will take it."

The smith smiled broadly. "A wise choice. I am sure you will wield it with honor and strength. It is a weapon meant for one destined for greatness."

CHAPTER NINE

Once Liu returned, he ordered the Chosen back to their room. As they made their way through the hall, the weight of the sword in its sheath at Kai's side felt both daunting and exhilarating. She couldn't help but steal glances at the weapon, all while the words of the white-haired smith echoed in her mind.

Back in their chambers, Kai stood by her bed, watching the other Chosen as they sat together, whispering and occasionally looking in her direction. She huffed loudly, and when Jiro looked at her, she met his gaze.

"If you are going to talk ill of me, do it to my face and not like cowards." The words poured from her unbidden, and she was surprised at herself.

"We are talking about you, but not badly," Jiro replied. "We're discussing what is written about the Blooded One. I think you are the one the scrolls speak of."

"Blooded One?" Kai asked. "Is this about the dragon blood? I told that man I've never seen or touched a dragon!"

"Calm down," Jiro soothed. "It's a good thing if you're this person."

"Not really," another of the Chosen said. It was a boy named Kazu. "The writings could mean she is evil."

Kai scowled. "What are you talking about? I'm not evil, and I'm not whatever the Blooded One is."

"You don't know what the Blooded One is?" Jiro asked. "Everyone knows."

"She wouldn't know because she's not like us," Kazu said. "She's a noble."

Jiro broke away from the group and came to stand beside Kai. "You really don't know what is written?"

"No."

"Can I tell you?"

Kai shrugged. "Sure."

"It's not exactly a prophecy, but it kind of is. It says that someone who has been bathed in a dragon's blood will save the empire."

"*Tsk*, that's not what it says." They both turned to see Siran. She was holding her hand close to her chest.

"Are you all right?" Kai asked. "I'm so sorry."

"It wasn't your fault. It's not like you made the sword hurt me... did you?"

"Of course not!"

Siran smirked. "I know. It was a joke. My hand is fine. The pain was intense, but the healers put some sort of balm on it and it feels normal now."

"I'm glad you're not hurt," Kai said.

"Me too. Why are you letting Jiro fill your head with nonsense?"

"It's not nonsense," Jiro protested.

"Some might argue otherwise. Either way, the scrolls do not say the Blooded One will save the empire. And the scrolls don't use the term Blooded One. That's something zealots came up with."

"Everyone uses it," Jiro said defensively.

"I'm not judging you," Siran replied. "I'm just saying."

"I've never heard of this prophecy or whatever," Kai said. "What is it?"

"I'm not surprised. Commoners latch onto it because they think this mythical person is going to lift them out of poverty or something. As nobles, we don't put our faith in fables."

Jiro glowered at Siran but said nothing.

"It's a poem of sorts," Siran continued. "I remember it because my grandmother used to recite it to me. How does it start again... Oh, that's right.

> *When the blood of a dragon stains the pure,*
> *A child shall rise to endure.*
> *With flames that dance and shadows that sprawl,*
> *This harbinger shall heed destiny's call.*
> *Upon their ascent, the world shall see,*
> *A dawn of hope or a night of misery.*
> *For in the heart of the dragon's kin,*
> *Lies the power to save or sin.*"

Kai digested the words as best as she could, but it didn't make any sense to her. "I don't see the connection," she said.

"Of course not. You have common sense, which isn't so common with them," Siran nodded her head toward the others. "You'd think it would be. I mean, it's in the title commoner." She scoffed.

Kai smiled. She didn't agree with Siran putting people down, but she did find that last bit humorous.

"We're not stupid because we believe in something different than you," Jiro said. "Some of us have put our hope into something higher than ourselves."

Before Siran could respond, the door to their chamber swung open and Liu strode in with the other guards.

"Drakka have been spotted in the woods," he announced. "Master Satoshi feels it is best to hold the ceremony now and then send you all to Dangju for training. Take a moment to pack to your things, then meet us in the courtyard."

Kai felt some relief when the guards left. Liu hadn't mentioned her sword or the strange prophecy, which meant he probably didn't believe in it any more than she did. She focused on the urgency of the moment and opened the chest at the end of her bed, gathering her belongings. The other Chosen rushed about frantically, their voices a chorus of concern.

Once everyone was prepared, they exited the room and made their way to the courtyard. An announcement must have been made because there was a large crowd already gathered. The air was tense with anticipation, and Kai's stomach churned at the realization that life as she knew it was about to change forever.

A short rectangular platform had been erected in the center of the courtyard, and Master Satoshi was there waiting for them. The Chosen filed onto the platform and lined up in an orderly row, facing the crowd. Kai looked for her parents and spotted them to her left. They didn't wave, but she could tell by their expressions they were proud of her.

Master Satoshi raised his hand for silence, and the buzz of the crowd gradually hushed. His voice carried through the courtyard with authority, each word echoing off the stone walls.

"The Ceremony of Oaths is a sacred ceremony, created by our ancestors to honor the bond between dragon and rider. A person is not Chosen based on birthright or merit, but by destiny. These men and women stand before you as a symbol of hope and strength, chosen by their dragons to protect our empire from the encroaching darkness."

He paused and looked down the line of Chosen, his gaze lingering on Kai who stood at the end of the line. She felt his stare and looked at him, meeting his eyes briefly before he turned his attention back to the crowd.

"For centuries, we have lived under the threat of the Drakka, but every day, hope blossoms. Every new Chosen is a promise for an end to our plight. They fight—we *all* fight— to bring an end to the Drakka."

Kai could feel the weight of Master Satoshi's words pressing down on her, the gravity of their calling settling deep in her bones. She glanced at the others standing beside her. Their faces were a mixture of determination and fear. They were all so young to be burdened with such responsibility, one far greater than themselves.

"Let us remember the sacrifices made by those who came before us and honor their legacy with our actions," Master Satoshi continued. "The strength of our empire lies not in the grandeur of our cities, but in the courage and unity of its people."

The courtyard fell into a solemn silence. Kai's heart thundered in her chest. This was it. She was finally going to meet her dragon. It had long been a day she dreaded, but now her soul longed for it.

"Let us begin the Ceremony of Oaths."

CHAPTER TEN

The sound of beating wings echoed through the air as the dragons that had arrived the night before soared over the walls, landing behind the platform. They were a magnificent sight, their scales shimmering in the sunlight. They were much larger than Kai expected, even after glimpsing them previously. She could feel the power emanating from them, a primal force that made her heart race with fear and excitement.

Her emotions were mirrored by the crowd, who murmured among themselves. The dragons trumpeted their presence, and Kai could feel her clothes vibrating from the sound. As one, the Chosen fell onto their knees and bowed their heads, paying homage to their more powerful counterparts.

"Siran," Master Satoshi called out. "Rise and approach your dragon."

Siran stood, her steps confident as she walked towards the dragon that awaited her. The dragon was a regal creature with scales as red as rubies, contrasting sharply against the dark colors of the stone wall behind it. She stopped a few feet short, and the dragon leaned down, putting its face inches from Siran's.

Master Satoshi joined them, holding a golden bowl and a dagger. Siran held her hand out, and Master Satoshi ran the blade across her palm. Kai admired Siran for not making a sound or flinching. The red dragon raised its front left leg and Master Satoshi gently lifted one of its scales, cutting the leathery skin underneath. He collected drops of blood from them both into the bowl, then stirred it with the dagger.

Kai waited expectantly, but nothing happened. Master Satoshi carried the bowl to a brazier and poured the blood into it. The flames roared upward, changing briefly to the same color as the dragon's scales, then returned to normal. Master Satoshi walked back to Siran's side.

"Speak the vows," he said.

Siran straightened and spoke loudly for all to hear. "By the sacred flame and the ancient bond we share, I vow to uphold the honor of our ancestors, to protect our lands and its people with courage and wisdom. With my dragon as my guide and my strength, I pledge my life to the guardianship of our realm, now and for all eternity."

The dragon lifted its head and turned its attention to Master Satoshi. Projecting its thoughts, it spoke to everyone who was present. *By the breath of fire and the skies we soar, I vow to honor our ancient bond, to protect our lands and its creatures with might and grace. With my rider as my heart and my spirit, I pledge my life to the guardianship of our realm, now and for all eternity.*

Then together, Siran and her dragon said, "As one soul in two bodies, we vow to stand as guardians of our world. In unity, strength, and unwavering loyalty, for the light of our bond shall guide us, now and forevermore."

Kai was in awe. The dragon's voice was deep and gruff, unlike anything she imagined. Was her dragon's voice the same?

"You are all witness to the Oaths," Master Satoshi said. "Let no one question their devotion to the empire, nor to one another. Now they will take to the sky for their first flight."

The red dragon lowered itself to the ground, and Siran used the ridges of his scales to climb up his shoulder, settling herself between his shoulder blades. There was no saddle, no straps, nothing at all to keep her from falling off the dragon's back. Kai frowned, wondering how she would stay put. Siran leaned forward, practically lying down, and grabbed hold of the scales on the dragon's neck.

With a mighty leap, the beast was in the air, his massive wings stirring up dirt in the courtyard, carrying them upward. Kai watched in awe as Siran and her dragon soared together, their figures becoming smaller against the vast expanse of the sky. The crowd erupted into cheers, their voices carrying up to the heavens.

As she gazed up at them, a mix of emotions swirled within Kai. There was a pang of envy at the strength of Siran's bond with her dragon, and an underlying fear of the unknown that lay ahead. Would she and her dragon be as majestic together? Would they form a connection as strong and unbreakable? Her eyes slowly moved from the sky to the gray dragon.

Can you hear me? she asked, trying to project her voice through their bond.

Silence met her question, and if the dragon could hear her, it gave no physical indication. She considered what Master Satoshi told her and forced her doubts away. Once they completed the Oaths, she was confident their bond would strengthen enough to communicate with one another.

Eventually the red dragon came back into view, circling above the crowd before landing in his original spot. Siran leaped down to the ground, her face flushed with pride and exhilaration. Master Satoshi nodded at her, a smile tugging at the corners of his lips.

"There are few things that compare to flying with your dragon," he said. "We are honored to witness your Oaths. Siran Himura, you are no longer Chosen. You are now Sworn."

The crowd roared with excitement once more, and Kai felt a sudden urge to cry. She finally understood the significance of the Ceremony of Oaths. Even though rider and dragon were already bonded, there was something incredibly emotional about the ritual itself. She managed to hold back the tears, and as Siran returned to her place among the Chosen, Kai smiled at her.

"Ichiro," Master Satoshi said. "Rise and approach your dragon."

Ichiro did as commanded, striding across the platform and onto the cobbled stones to stand before an enormous blue dragon whose scales glittered like sapphires. Its eyes locked onto Ichiro, and a sense of recognition passed between them. Without hesitation, Ichiro reached out his hand, palm open, and the dragon leaned down to nuzzle his fingertips gently. It was a moment of pure connection, a silent understanding that needed no words.

Master Satoshi stepped forward with the golden bowl and dagger once more, cleaned and ready. With practiced ease, he cut their flesh and drew blood, mixing it in the bowl before igniting it in the brazier. The flames danced in a mesmerizing display before settling into a steady glow. Ichiro and his dragon stood face to face as they recited their vows, their voices intertwining in a harmonious echo that resonated through the courtyard.

As they finished, the blue dragon dipped its head in a solemn bow, and Ichiro placed his hand on its massive snout, rubbing the scales.

"You are all witness to the Oaths," Master Satoshi repeated. "Let no one question their devotion to the empire, nor to one another. Now they will take to the sky for their first flight."

The blue dragon knelt before Ichiro, and he clambered onto its back. With a powerful thrust of its wings, the dragon launched itself into the air, carrying Ichiro aloft. The crowd watched in hushed awe as they circled above just as Siran and her dragon had done moments before.

The ceremony continued in the same fashion, with Jiro going after his brother. He was bonded to a green dragon whose scales were like polished jade. Next was Kazu, followed by Reika. Kai watched each ritual with a mix of reverence and excitement. Eleven Chosen were now Sworn, and Kai was the only who one remained.

It was finally her turn.

"Kai, rise and approach your dragon."

Kai felt her heart leap into her throat as all eyes turned to her. The importance of the moment settled upon her shoulders, and for a brief instant, doubt gnawed at the edges of her resolve. She took a deep breath and walked towards the great gray dragon, her steps faltering slightly in her nervousness. The dragon regarded her with eyes that seemed to pierce through her very soul, assessing her with a gaze that was both intimidating and strangely comforting.

Master Satoshi joined them, his presence reassuring as he performed the ritual of the blood. Kai gritted her teeth against the pain of the cut on her palm, willing herself to remain stoic like Siran had. The dragon watched intently, a rumble reverberating in its chest. Master Satoshi collected its blood next, and the golden bowl shimmered in the sunlight as he approached the brazier.

With a steady hand, he poured the blood into the flames. The fire erupted in a dazzling display of silver light, flickering and dancing with an ethereal glow. Kai felt a surge of energy course through her, a tingling sensation that pulled at the edges of her *ki*. Her dragon was a male. She wasn't sure how she knew that. She just... knew.

"Speak the vows," Master Satoshi instructed.

She stared at the dragon, the words suddenly fleeing her memory. She'd learned the vow when she was young, had repeated it countless times in her short life. Why now, at the most important moment of her life, did the words elude her grasp? Master Satoshi cleared his throat, drawing her attention. His stern gaze jolted something within her, and the words came rushing back. She drew a steadying breath.

"By the sacred flame and the ancient bond we share, I vow to uphold the honor of our ancestors, to protect our lands and its people with courage and wisdom. With my dragon as my guide and my strength, I pledge my life to the guardianship of our realm, now and for all eternity."

The dragon regarded her for a moment before leaning closer. He sniffed the air around her, his warm breath washing over her face. Kai could feel the weight of his presence and it sent a chill down her spine. Lifting his head, he projected his voice for everyone to hear.

This is not my rider.

CHAPTER ELEVEN

Kai's heart plummeted at the dragon's words, and a cold dread settled in the pit of her stomach. The revelation hung heavy in the air, stirring a wave of murmurs and gasps through the crowd. Kai's pulse pounded in her ears, her mind struggling to comprehend the dragon's words.

"This cannot be," Master Satoshi declared, his voice carrying his authority despite a flicker of uncertainty in his eyes. "The bond is predetermined by the ancient rites. There can be no mistake."

The dragon huffed, puffs of smoke escaping its nostrils as it regarded Kai with an intensity that made her feel exposed, vulnerable. She sensed a ripple of unease pass through the Sworn behind her, their whispers blending into a dissonant hum that resonated in her bones. She stole a glance at Master Satoshi, searching for some sign of reassurance or explanation in his expression, but his features remained stoic and unreadable.

"I am Kai Lin," she said, her words sounding feeble even to her own ears. "Daughter of Ryoko Lin and Sho Lin. My mother received the Sign when I was in her womb. I *am* your rider."

You are not.

Before anyone could speak further, a figure emerged from the outskirts of the courtyard. Clad in dark robes that billowed around them like shadows given form, the newcomer strode purposefully towards the platform where Kai and the dragon were. A hood obscured their features, casting a veil of mystery over their identity as they drew closer, but Kai caught a glimpse of glacial blue eyes. The stranger's presence exuded an otherworldly aura, a sense of power that commanded attention.

As the stranger reached the foot of the platform, they raised a hand and pushed back their hood, revealing a face that was both familiar and foreign to Kai. It was a face she had seen countless times in the mirror... her own.

Confusion and disbelief warred within Kai as she tried to make sense of what she saw. Was this a dark spirit disguising itself as her? Or had she fallen under some sort of curse? The woman, who appeared to be her but also not quite, extended her hand towards the gray dragon. He nuzzled his snout against her affectionately.

The woman's eyes swept over the gathering, landing on Master Satoshi. "The bond between dragon and rider is not always as straightforward as tradition dictates."

"Who are you to interrupt the sacred ceremony?"

A ghost of a smile pulled at the woman's lips. "I am Akuhara Lin, daughter of Ryoko Lin and Sho Lin, and I have come to claim my dragon."

A stunned silence settled over the courtyard. Master Satoshi's brows were scrunched in disbelief.

"Impossible," Kai whispered. A surge of conflicting emotions coursed through her—confusion, anger, and a deep-seated fear. How could this woman claim to share her bloodline and lineage? Was this some elaborate ruse, a deception woven with dark magic to disrupt the ritual? And yet the dragon himself said Kai was not his rider.

"Explain yourselves," Master Satoshi demanded, glancing from Akuhara to Kai.

She speaks true, the gray dragon rumbled. *Akuhara is my rider.*

Akuhara climbed onto the dragon's back, a smug expression on her face. Master Satoshi stood still, clearly confused. Finally, he looked at Kai, anger burning in his eyes.

"Did you lie about being Chosen?"

"No! I would never dishonor myself or my family."

"Take her to the dungeon," he commanded. "Her fate will be decided after the ceremony." He turned to Akuhara. "You must complete the Oaths."

Liu came to stand near Kai, and he grabbed onto her arm with a firm grip. She looked at him pleadingly, but he wouldn't look her in the eyes.

"There's no need," Akuhara replied. "I do not fight for the empire."

Master Satoshi sputtered. "Riders serve *only* the empire. If you do not fight for the empire, who do you fight for?"

Akuhara laughed briefly, then her expression turned serious. "I fight for the Drakka."

Horrified whispers erupted among the crowd of onlookers. Soldiers drew their swords, and Master Satoshi clenched his jaw. "Blasphemy!"

A horn blared, followed by the ringing of the bell tower. The silence of the courtyard turned into chaos as panic spread through the crowd like wildfire. The Sworn looked to Master Satoshi for guidance.

"You will all be witnesses," Akuhara shouted. "The empire will burn!"

With that, the gray dragon took to the sky. People scrambled in all directions, cries of fear and disbelief mingling with the ominous tolling of the bell tower. Kai found herself frozen in place, her mind reeling. Her parents would have the answers. They could explain to Master Satoshi that this was all a mistake. The Sworn would hunt down the doppelganger, and Kai would get her dragon back.

"Come with me," Liu said, guiding her through the turmoil toward the castle.

"My parents. They were in the crowd. They can—"

"That's the least of our worries right now. Didn't you hear the bell? We're under attack."

Kai looked over her shoulder, trying to spot her parents. They were nowhere in sight. She prayed they were safe and allowed herself to be led by Liu. Master Satoshi, trailed by the new Sworn, followed them inside the castle.

"Once the dragons are saddled, you will all flee to Dangju," he said. "I sent word to them days ago informing them of your arrival. You will train there, and report back here once you are done. Do not stop once you leave these walls. Go straight to Dangju."

"Yes, Master," they said in unison.

"As for you," he continued, looking at Kai, "I demand answers to your deception."

"I have deceived no one," she replied. "My parents are here. You can ask them, and they will tell you the same."

Master Satoshi looked at Liu. "Go find them."

Liu offered a quick bow and rushed off.

"Can we not stay and fight?" Siran asked. "I have trained with a sword most of my life. There is nothing anyone can teach me in Dangju."

"There is more to being a rider than wielding a blade," Master Satoshi answered. "You must learn about your bond and how to strengthen it. You will go to Dangju as I have commanded."

Siran lowered her head in submission, but Kai knew she was not happy. She was a warrior, and warriors did not run from battle. Master Satoshi turned his attention back to Kai. His accusation hung over her like a dark cloud, but she had spoken the truth. She clenched her fists, fighting against the urge to lash out in frustration at the injustice of it all.

Liu returned with her parents in tow. Tears streamed down her mother's face, and her father was pale as though he were going to be ill.

"Kai's fate hangs by a thread," Master Satoshi said to them. "Speak honestly with me and she may yet be spared. Did you receive the Sign?"

Ryoko nodded. "I did."

"Describe it to me."

"At the Binding, I laid my hands on several eggs and felt nothing. When I touched the last one, warmth spread through my stomach, and I felt a kick. The Inquisitor who was present confirmed it."

"And you do not know this Akuhara?"

"I am... not sure."

"What do you mean?"

Ryoko choked back a sob. "I bore two children in my womb, but one was stillborn."

Master Satoshi frowned. "You had a first born that died upon birth?"

"No. I gave birth to twins."

CHAPTER TWELVE

Kai felt as though she had been punched in the chest. Twins? Her mother had never mentioned anything about that.

"I'm sorry," Ryoko said, looking at her. "I should have told you."

"That doesn't answer my question," Master Satoshi growled. "What does a stillborn baby have to do with anything?"

"You saw the resemblance, as we all did," Sho answered. "She looked just like Kai. My wife thinks—*we* think it could be her."

Master Satoshi rubbed his hands over his face. "You said yourself the baby was stillborn. How could Akuhara be your child?"

"I know how it sounds, my lord, even to my own ears," Ryoko said. "And yet, she is a reflection of Kai. It is her. I know it."

"How do you know?"

"Mother's intuition."

"Was she left with a healer?" Master Satoshi asked.

"The Drakka attacked our city, and I went into labor," Ryoko said, her gaze distant as she recounted the terrifying moment. Kai could tell that she was reliving it all in her

61

mind. "A dragon was struck in the sky overhead..." She paused, and Sho squeezed her hand reassuringly. "Its blood splattered all over me. We were almost to the carriage, but the pain was too much."

Ryoko's sobs echoed throughout the hall as she covered her face with her hands. Kai felt a pang in her heart as she watched her mother cry. Her own eyes welled up with tears, and one escaped, sliding down her cheek.

"The first one came easily, but something was wrong," Sho continued for her. "She was pale, and she wasn't breathing. We did everything we could, but... she was lifeless. Then Kai was born, and we had to escape. The Drakka were everywhere."

"They took her from me," Ryoko said, shuddering. "I should have fought them for her body, but I couldn't risk all of our lives for... for..."

"A corpse," Master Satoshi offered softly. "I understand."

"We left her behind," Ryoko whispered, her face haunted. "We left her behind."

Kai envisioned it all within her mind. She didn't blame her mother for leaving a child behind. As Master Satoshi said, it was a lost cause, and it would be foolish to endanger the living for the sake of the dead.

"She *is* the Blooded One," Jiro said to his brother. Kai had almost forgotten the Sworn were still present.

"There is much to consider," Master Satoshi said, ignoring Jiro's comment.

The ground trembled as a crash echoed in the courtyard. Master Satoshi exchanged glances with Liu, and the guard rushed away. He returned a moment later, his face flushed.

"The walls have been breached!"

"Impossible," Master Satoshi breathed. "Get to your dragons, now!"

The Sworn scrambled toward the courtyard, all except for Siran. She remained rooted in place. Kai looked from Master

Satoshi to her parents. Her mother was still crying, but she seemed more collected now.

"Secure yourselves here in the castle," Master Satoshi told them. Turning to Kai, he stared at her in silence, his mouth twitching slightly. "You can't stay here. It's not safe without your dragon."

"I can take her to Tatenagawa," Liu said.

The shrine? Kai's brows furrowed in confusion.

"My lord!" A breathless soldier sprinted through the hall toward them. "We're surrounded! The Drakka—I've never seen so many!"

"You won't make it ten yards beyond the wall," Master Satoshi said grimly.

"Not on foot," Siran replied. "I'll take her to Tatenagawa."

"You have your orders, Siran. I will not repeat them."

"I'll take her to Tatenagawa, then go to Dangju. You can't spare anyone else, and even if you could, the others are too soft. I can take her."

"She is my charge," Liu said. "I will take her."

"You don't have a dragon," Siran countered.

"We don't have time for this," Master Satoshi snapped. "Can your dragon hold three?"

Siran's confidence wavered. "Does he have a choice?"

The sounds of battle erupted outside—the clash of metal, the roar of dragons, the screams of soldiers.

"Go," Master Satoshi conceded.

Kai embraced her mother tightly. "I will see you again," she promised.

"I'm sorry," her mother whispered.

"Don't be. It was painful for you to talk about it even now. I understand." She released her mother and turned to her father. He gave her a sad smile.

"May your blade serve you well," he said.

"You must go now," Master Satoshi urged.

Kai quickly hugged her father, then rushed toward the courtyard, following Siran. Liu was beside her, his blade drawn.

"Why are we going to Tatenagawa?" Kai asked.

"To see Kokoro," Liu replied.

"Who is that?"

"She is an elder dragon. If anyone can discern what happened here, it's her."

The three of them crossed the courtyard to where Siran's dragon waited. As they approached, the ground quaked beneath their feet as a portion of the wall collapsed. The air was thick with the acrid scent of smoke and the cries of soldiers engaged in combat.

Siran climbed onto her dragon's back, taking the frontmost position. Kai looked at Liu, who motioned for her to go next. She did so, and Liu sat behind her. Only Siran fit within the saddle, leaving Kai and Liu to sit on the rough scales of the dragon's back.

"Hold on tight," Siran said.

Kai obeyed, wrapping her arms securely around Siran's waist while Liu held onto Kai. With a powerful leap, the dragon launched into the sky, its wings beating rhythmically as it ascended higher and higher. From above, they could see the full extent of the battle unfolding below. The Drakka forces surged against the castle walls like a relentless tide.

Kai's heart raced as they soared through the air. The feeling of flight was exhilarating, but it was tainted by the events unfolding below. She worried for her parents. Ikje had never been attacked by Drakka before due to the strength of its defenses, but as she watched the dark wave of creatures overtake the walls, a chill ran down her spine.

She turned her gaze from the battle and offered a prayer to her ancestors.

CHAPTER THIRTEEN

Kai focused on the landscape rushing beneath them, the fields and forests blurring together as they flew toward Tatenagawa. The wind whipped against her face, tousling her hair wildly as they cut through the air. The dragon carried them swiftly, effortlessly gliding over the terrain below.

As they approached the sacred grounds of Tatenagawa, Kai marveled at the natural beauty of the area. The lush greenery, the tranquil ponds, and the ancient trees all exuded a sense of peace and serenity. Siran's dragon descended, landing on the banks of a river where it met the ocean.

Kai dismounted after Siran, followed by Liu. The ground felt oddly solid beneath her feet after being in the air. A winding path lined with statues led to a grove of cherry blossom trees. The air was filled with the soft murmur of the river and the scent of blooming flowers. A sense of reverence washed over Kai.

"Come with me," Liu said.

"What about Siran?"

"She has her orders from Master Satoshi. She is to go to Dangju."

"If she leaves, we have no way to get back," Kai said. "What if the elder cannot help? We'll be stuck here."

"We can travel on foot if we must."

Kai looked at Siran.

"My dragon needs rest. Once he is ready, we will go. If you are not back by then, I shall see you when you return to Ikje."

Liu led Kai through the grove. Shafts of sunlight filtered through the canopy, painting patterns on the moss-covered ground. Kai noticed small shrines tucked among the trees and assumed they were offerings left by visitors. The atmosphere was tranquil, and the faint scent of incense drifted on the wind.

On the other side of the grove, a clearing opened up, revealing a grand structure. It was a temple of ancient design, its wooden beams weathered by time yet standing strong and proud. The entrance was flanked by two stone dragons that looked as if they were guarding the temple.

Liu pushed open the heavy wooden doors, and they entered a dimly lit hallway adorned with intricate murals depicting scenes of dragons soaring through the skies and warriors engaged in battle. The air was laced with the scent of sandalwood and old parchment. They walked in silence, their footsteps echoing on the polished wood floor. The hallway led them to a vast open chamber where a figure awaited them.

"Welcome," a voice greeted. The figure was cloaked in flowing robes that seemed to shift and shimmer with a life of their own. It was an elderly woman with eyes that gleamed with ancient wisdom. Her hair was silver, cascading down her back like a waterfall of moonlight. She gazed at Kai and Liu with a knowing smile, as if she had been expecting them.

"We come seeking the guidance of the elder," Liu said.

The woman's smile deepened as she studied them with a piercing gaze, her eyes seeming to see through the very core of their beings. She nodded slowly, acknowledging Liu's words.

"I had hoped this day would come before my time ended." Her voice was melodic, resonating with a power that seemed to vibrate the very air around them. "The wind whispers of you." Her eyes studied Kai. "The one who is both Chosen and not Chosen."

"As he said, we are here to see the elder," Kai said. "Will she grant us an audience?"

The woman laughed softly. "Would you rather I take my dragon form? You could not look upon me if I did. Humans are such soft creatures, even more so now than they once were."

"You are Kokoro?" Liu asked.

Kokoro nodded sagely. "I am."

"We need your help," Kai said. "Ikje is under siege by the Drakka."

"That is not why you are here. Not truly, is it? No, I think not. The wind did not lie."

Kai looked at Liu, who offered a slight nod.

"Someone stole my dragon."

"A dragon has free will," Kokoro replied. "If your dragon left, it did so of its own mind. Tell me what happened."

Kai relayed the events of the Ceremony of Oaths to her, and how her dragon said she was not his rider. She hesitated sharing her mother's revelation about birthing twins, but Liu pressed her, and she told the elder everything, including the fact her mother had been drenched in dragon's blood. Kokoro listened intently, her expression unreadable as she absorbed the tale. When Kai finished speaking, there was only silence in the chamber. Kokoro closed her eyes briefly, as if listening to some unseen force, before opening them once more.

"The threads of the world are tangled, and the path ahead is shrouded in darkness," Kokoro replied cryptically. "The balance that has long existed is unraveling. What do you know of the Accord?"

Kai shook her head. "I've never heard of it."

"And you?" Kokoro asked Liu.

"It is not familiar to me."

"That doesn't surprise me. Mankind's memory is short. Do you know how the bond came to be, or where the Drakka came from?"

Kai and Liu exchanged looks of confusion. They shook their heads in unison, prompting Kokoro to let out a soft sigh.

"The Accord is an ancient pact forged between dragons and humans centuries ago. It bound our fates together, ensuring balance and harmony in the world."

"What do you mean?" Kai asked. "Have we not always been bound to each other?"

"Before the Accord, our races were enemies. I am old enough to remember those days." Kokoro frowned. "That was a dark time. Humans are a weak species, but they outnumbered us. We called for a truce and invited the emperor to speak with us."

Kai found it hard to imagine being enemies with a dragon. They were the epitome of strength and power. The notion of dragons and humans standing on opposite sides of a battlefield seemed more akin to a fanciful tale than a history lesson.

"The emperor at the time was a wise man," Kokoro continued, her voice filled with something Kai couldn't quite place. "He saw the value in forging an alliance rather than waging war, but the price of his demand was steep. He felt dragons were too powerful, and we were forced to shed a great portion of our strength. As a result, dragons became smaller and less formidable."

Kai listened intently, her mind trying to grasp the implications of what Kokoro was revealing. The very fabric of their history was shifting, revealing secrets long buried in the sands of time.

"I cannot imagine dragons being larger than they are now," she said.

"I could show you, but I fear my transformation would burn the eyes from your skull."

"What of the Drakka? Did dragons and humans not fight them as well?"

"The Drakka did not exist," Kokoro replied. "The Accord changed the world, binding us to you in ways that are deeper than you can fathom. Some of my brethren dissented, rejecting the idea of being diminished, of bowing to human will." The elder's eyes glinted with sorrow.

"The Drakka are the remnants of my brethren who refused to abide by the terms of the Accord. With our power diminished, it had to go somewhere. It filled them until they were corrupted, becoming something entirely different. There must always be balance in the world, and the Drakka are the result of the balance correcting itself."

Kai could hardly believe what she was hearing. "The Drakka are dragons? They don't look like dragons at all."

"They once were, but as I said, they were corrupted. Now they are creatures bent on devastation. But this knowledge leads us back to you."

"Me?"

"Do you know what is written in the ancient scrolls?"

Kai shook her head. "I am not the one they speak of. I have never touched the blood of a dragon."

"Perhaps not, but it has touched you. Your mother confirmed it to you."

Kai opened her mouth to argue but as the realization settled over her, the words died in her throat. The weight of Kokoro's words bore down on Kai like a crushing wave, causing her chest to tighten. The revelation that she was somehow entwined in ancient pacts and prophecies left her reeling. She glanced at Liu, searching for a steadying presence in the swirling chaos of her thoughts. His expression mirrored her own; shock, fear, and emotions she couldn't put words to.

Kokoro's gaze lingered on Kai, the silver in her hair catching the light of the chamber like strands of moonlight woven into her being.

"Never has a dragon bonded with more than one human at once, yet the one who chose you and your sister has somehow done so. It seems your twin's connection is stronger to him than your own, but you are still Chosen. The prophecy has long been a contention among the humans. Some see it as a portent of doom, while others see it as their salvation."

"Which is it?" Kai asked, afraid to know.

"It is both."

"I don't understand. How can something be both evil and good?"

"You and your twin are two sides of the same coin. One embraces the darkness while the other shines in the light. The prophecy is not one side or the other, it is both combined."

Kai considered the elder's words. Something her mother said came back to her. "Why would the Drakka take my sister?" The words felt odd coming out of her mouth. She'd been led to believe she was an only child her entire life. "My parents thought she was dead. Why would the Drakka take a corpse?"

"The Drakka know the prophecy," Kokoro replied. "Deep down, they are dragons, and it was a dragon who penned the words. When they saw your mother covered in dragon's blood, they knew the ancient words had come to pass."

"But the Drakka are mindless creatures," Kai protested. "They couldn't know that."

Kokoro laughed. "Is that what humans tell themselves these days? The Drakka are disorganized, I will grant you.

Discord is their very nature, which means they do not work together, but if someone were to unite them…”

“My sister,” Kai whispered.

“Yes. The Drakka must have raised her as their own, and now she leads them. That is the only explanation for what you say is happening at Ikje. She is the dark side of the coin.”

“And I am expected to be the light side?”

“I do not expect you to be anything,” Kokoro said. “But you will have to make a choice. The balance that has long existed is unraveling, and it will correct itself one way or another.”

“How can I do anything when I don’t control the bond? The dragon said himself that Akuhara was his rider. And since I am also bound to the dragon, she can probably hear my thoughts even now.”

“Perhaps, though I do not suspect the bond works that way. It is impossible to know since this has never happened before, but it does not matter.”

“Why not?”

“Because you can sever your connection with him and forge a new bond.”

CHAPTER FOURTEEN

Kai stared at Kokoro, her brows furrowed. "I thought once a bond was formed, it only ended upon death?"

"That is usually how a bond ends, but as part of the Accord, a human reserves the right to sever it."

"What happens when the bond is severed?"

"The bond would break, and both you and the dragon would feel pain. Since you are not as connected to him as your twin, I think the pain would be lessened. You would then be free to bond with a new dragon."

"How would I bond with a new dragon? The Binding happens when we are both unborn."

"The dragon you would bond with is... unique. She is unhatched, but she has long been ready to enter the world."

The choice before her weighed heavily on her shoulders. The revelation that she could sever her bond and forge a new one with an unhatched dragon left her feeling both hopeful and terrified.

"What would I need to do to sever the bond?"

"It is not an easy task," Kokoro replied. "To sever a bond with a dragon requires great sacrifice. You must be willing to give up a part of yourself, to let go of something precious to you."

Kai's mind raced as she tried to think of what she could possibly offer. What was so important to her that ridding herself of it would be a sacrifice? Even as she considered that question, deep down she knew. She looked at Liu, who stood there silently. She wanted to ask him for guidance, but he could never understand what her choice entailed. The image of her parents came to mind, and she knew that even if her decision only saved them, it would be worth the cost.

"I will do it," she said, her voice steady despite the roiling emotions within her.

"You have a brave heart, Kai. You must go to the sacred grounds where the Accord was made. There, you will find the egg and undergo the Ritual of Severance."

"Where can I find this place?"

"It is not far from here," Kokoro answered. "I will take you there."

"I will come with you," Liu said. "Until she is Sworn, she is under my protection."

"Very well."

"We should let Siran know in case she's waiting." Kai glanced at Liu, expecting him to be annoyed that the woman was not following her orders.

"She is gone," Kokoro said.

"How do you know?"

"I felt her dragon's presence leave the area."

"Oh." Kai was disappointed, but she didn't know why. Siran had her own path to follow. Perhaps it was because she was the closest thing to a friend Kai had ever had.

"Before we go, we will eat. The journey isn't long, but it is arduous and you will need your strength for the ritual."

Kokoro treated them to a delicious meal of roasted rabbit, sweet potatoes, and an herbal tea that was both soothing and invigorating. As they ate, Kokoro talked about the Accord. The more Kai learned, the more she realized there was much she didn't know. It also made her question why no one taught them about the Accord or the history of it. Kai considered Kokoro's words about the shortness of human memories, but she couldn't help feeling there was more to it than that.

Once they had all finished their meal, Kokoro led them out of the temple and through the grove, heading southeast to where the mountains loomed. As she had warned, the landscape was difficult to traverse. The path was rocky and uneven, and the dense forest surrounding them seemed to press in on them from all sides. The air was thick with the scent of damp leaves and earth, and the occasional rustle of small animals scurrying away revealed their presence.

Kai found herself focusing on each step, her mind racing with thoughts of the ritual ahead. They walked for several hours until, finally, they reached a clearing at the base of the mountains surrounded by ancient, towering trees that seemed to stretch towards the sky, their branches woven together like a natural cathedral. The dark entrance of a cave stood ominously before them.

"This is it," Kokoro said quietly, as if her voice could disturb the sanctity of the place.

Kai swallowed hard, feeling a strange mix of dread and anticipation.

"Are you sure about this?" Liu asked, the concern evident in his voice.

Was she? No, not really, but that didn't matter. They'd come this far, and it wouldn't be right to turn away now. She nodded.

"Come," Kokoro beckoned.

As they entered the cave, the air grew cooler. The darkness swallowed them briefly before Kokoro spoke a word Kai didn't know and torches on the walls flared to life. She led them deeper into the cave, passing strange symbols carved upon the walls. The ceiling gradually grew lower, forcing them to stoop as they walked, and the ground was covered in a thick layer of leaves.

"Time has changed this tunnel," Kokoro said. "It used to be more accommodating."

Despite the light of the torches, the darkness seemed to pull at Kai, and she gripped the hilt of her sword for comfort, her heart racing. The cave curved inward, twisting and turning like a maze. Kokoro led them deeper still until the tunnel opened up into a vast chamber, hollowed out of the mountain's heart.

In the center sat a massive egg, its surface a deep shade of gold with iridescent markings that sparkled like stars against the blackness of the chamber. Kai's breath caught in her throat. It was the most beautiful thing she had ever seen. She couldn't tear her eyes away from it, and she could sense the dormant life pulsating from the egg. As they drew closer, Kai realized the egg towered over all of them. It seemed too large to belong to a dragon. She glanced at Liu, but his focus was captured by the golden egg.

"It's so big," Kai whispered.

"As I said, this dragon is unique. Now, to sever your bond, you will place your hands upon the egg and envision your *ki*. Find the connection that flows outward from it toward your dragon and cut it using your sacrifice as the blade."

Kai nodded and quietly approached the egg. The energy coming from the egg stirred, and she could feel something brush against her mind. Was this what her mother had experienced during the Binding? She pushed the thought away and laid her hands on the egg. The surface was smooth and radiated warmth.

Closing her eyes, she focused on her *ki*. In her mind's eye, she found the bond and pictured it as a glowing thread linking her to the gray dragon. With a deep breath, she summoned her courage. She had never wanted to be Chosen. Instead, she had wanted an easy life, one filled with children of her own. Tears stung her eyes as she imagined her motherhood as a blade and placed it against the thread. Steeling herself, she cut the bond.

A searing pain shot through her, causing her to gasp and lose her balance. Liu moved swiftly to support her, but Kokoro gestured for him to stay back.

"She must endure this on her own," she said.

Gritting her teeth, Kai pushed through the pain, focusing on cutting the bond cleanly and completely. The golden egg beneath her hands began to resonate with her efforts, its surface pulsating with a soft light. With one final surge of willpower, Kai felt the connection snap, causing a wave of agony to ripple through her entire being.

Her legs threatened to give out, but she clung stubbornly to her resolve, the darkness at the edge of her vision almost within reach. Through the storm of pain, she felt the egg begin to quiver. As the pain subsided, Kai started to breathe again, her hands trembling against the egg. She had done it. The bond was severed.

"Now forge the new bond," Kokoro urged.

Kai took a deep breath, her heart pounding in her chest. She knew what she had to do, but she couldn't shake the feeling of loss.

"How do I...?" she began, but Kokoro interrupted her.

"Feel the connection that pulses between you and the egg. Envision it as a stream of living energy, flowing from you to the egg and back again. Your *ki* is essential to forging the bond."

Kai felt the energy Kokoro spoke of. She closed her eyes and concentrated, visualizing her *ki*. She reached out with it, feeling it flow towards the egg. The connection took shape, a golden thread linking the two of them together.

The egg responded to her efforts, emitting a soft hum that seemed to resonate with the very depths of her soul. Kai could sense a presence awakening within the golden shell, a consciousness stirring to life. It was unlike anything she had ever experienced, a merging of minds that transcended words or thoughts.

In that moment of unity, Kai felt a surge of emotions wash over her—joy, acceptance, and a profound sense of belonging. The golden thread shimmered and brightened, signifying the strength of their connection. A wave of dizziness washed over her, and as her vision darkened, she could hear Liu's voice, distant and echoing.

CHAPTER FIFTEEN

As Kai's eyelids fluttered open, she found herself sprawled on the ground in front of the egg. She sat up and noticed Liu and Kokoro gazing down at her. Liu's face was creased with worry, while Kokoro's radiated a sense of pride.

"The Binding is complete," the elder said.

Kai looked at the egg. The energy pulsing from within it was no longer dormant. It was active, and she could feel a presence within her mind, almost like her conscience, yet it was separate from her.

"When will it hatch?" Kai asked.

As if in answer to her question, a soft rumble resonated from the egg. It grew in intensity until cracks spiderwebbed across the egg's surface, emitting a soft golden light that illuminated the chamber in a dazzling display. Kai watched in awe as the dragon hatchling emerged from the egg, its scales gleaming like molten gold. It was just as large as the ones from the ceremony.

The dragon blinked its large, brilliant blue eyes and fixed them on Kai with an expression that seemed to convey wisdom beyond its years. It extended its snout towards her, nuzzling her hand in a gesture of trust and companionship. Tears welled up in Kai's eyes as she realized the depth of the connection she now shared with this majestic creature. The dragon's presence in her mind felt both strange and comforting, like a familiar voice speaking to her from a place deep within her soul.

Kai reached out tentatively, running her hand along the dragon hatchling's scales, feeling the warmth that radiated from its body. It chirruped softly, a sound that tugged at Kai's heartstrings. She could sense the dragon's curiosity and intelligence, and a flash of images appeared within her mind, and she realized it was trying to communicate with her.

I am Kai Lin, she said, sending the words through their bond.

More images flashed through her mind's eye, but she couldn't decipher their meaning.

"She can't speak?" Kai asked, looking at Kokoro.

"Not yet. Much like a human, it takes time to grow. Your dragon will mature faster than other dragons, and through your bond, you will help her learn about our world."

"You said she was unique. What does that mean?"

Kokoro glanced at Liu, and Kai assumed she didn't want to answer in front of him. "Whatever you want to tell me you can say in front of him," Kai said. "I trust him."

"Very well. Your dragon is different because she is an elder."

"Like you?"

"Yes."

"That's forbidden," Liu said.

"I know. I was there when the Accord was written."

"Then why did you allow this?"

"There are countless reasons, but I will tell you the most important one." Kokoro's demeanor grew solemn. "I am the sole survivor of my species. Well, not anymore," she gestured towards the golden dragon. "But my days are numbered. I will dedicate the remainder of my life to training both of you.

When I am gone, your dragon will be the final elder. It will be her responsibility to ensure our kind lives on."

"You used me?" Kai's face flushed with heat, both in surprise and anger. Her dragon growled, mirroring her emotions.

"No. Dragons do not employ such tactics. You and your sister are the ones written of, but the prophecy is not for humans... it is for dragons. The Accord took our power, but you will give it back to us."

Taking a deep breath to steady herself, Kai reached out and gently stroked the dragon's scales. The bond between them pulsed with newfound energy, a connection that seemed to grow stronger with each passing moment. Despite the circumstances surrounding their union, Kai had a feeling deep down that she was meant to walk this path. Whether she wanted to was another matter entirely.

Fate or destiny had called upon her, that much was clear, and she couldn't deny the sense of purpose that stirred within her. As she looked into the wise blue eyes of her dragon companion, she knew that their fates were intertwined in ways she was only beginning to understand. She straightened, determination shining in her gaze.

"I cannot guarantee I will fulfill this prophecy, if I am even truly the one it speaks if, but I will do whatever I must to protect my dragon and both of our species," Kai said. The dragon regarded her with a knowing look, as if understanding the weight of her words. Kokoro smiled, the darkness leaving her expression.

"You have the heart of a true dragon rider. Remember, the bond between you and your dragon is not just about duty. It is about trust, understanding, and love." With those words lingering in the air, Kokoro turned to Liu. "You no longer need to protect her. She is my ward now, and no harm will come to her."

"I mean no insult, but I made an oath to defend the Chosen I am assigned to until my last breath or until they are Sworn. If I do not keep my oath, my words mean nothing and I have no honor."

"Your honor is not in question," Kokoro said softly, her voice full of compassion. "But sometimes, the path we tread deviates from the one we have set for ourselves. Kai's journey is no longer yours to safeguard. She has taken the first step towards fulfilling a destiny greater than any single oath. You are welcome to stay here while she trains, but they must grow their bond in solitude, away from prying eyes."

"I understand," Liu replied. "I will not pry nor get in the way of her training."

"Thank you." Kokoro turned her attention back to Kai. "There is much for you to learn, and time is of the essence. Your dragon is an elder, and while she carries the wisdom of our ancestors within her, you must learn to communicate with her, to understand her thoughts and feelings. This will not be easy, but I will guide you through the process."

Kai nodded. She was ready for the challenges that lay ahead, ready to forge a bond unlike any the world had ever seen before. The dragon chirruped softly, nudging her hand with its snout as if agreeing with her. Kai could feel the weight of responsibility settling on her shoulders, but for the first time in her life, she no longer felt like she was facing things alone.

"First things first," Kai said. "You need a name."

RICHARD FIERCE

ACOLYTE

BOUND BY BLOOD BOOK 2

CHAPTER ONE

Kai walked in the shadows of the great statues that loomed around the temple courtyard—dragons with furled wings and riders whose eyes were fixed on the horizon, seeing things that were lost to time. A gust of wind stirred the dust on the cobblestones, carrying with it the faint scent of smoke.

Ahead, Liu waited for her. His posture was relaxed but alert, and his sword hung loosely in his hand, the blade glinting in the early morning light of the sun. Kai could see the calmness in his eyes, the patience of a warrior who had seen countless battles. She drew her blade, and the metal sang as it came free of the scabbard, the sound sharp and clear in the stillness.

"Ready?" Liu asked. His tone was soft, but there was a hint of something more, an edge that told her this would not be an easy session. Kai nodded, mirroring his stance.

He moved first, a swift, fluid motion that brought his sword arcing toward her with precision. Kai met the strike with her own blade, the clash of metal ringing out through the courtyard. The impact reverberated up Kai's arm, but she held firm, pushing back against Liu's strength.

They moved in a dance of steel, each strike and parry a show of skill. Liu was faster, more experienced, but Kai had her owns strengths. She was learning to anticipate his moves, to read the subtle shifts in his stance that signaled his next attack.

"Very good," Liu said. "Don't just react. Think ahead. Where will my next strike come from?"

Kai tightened her grip on the hilt of her sword. She saw the flicker in Liu's eyes, the slight shift of his weight, and she moved, bringing her sword up to block his next strike. Their blades locked, and for a moment, they were face to face.

"Better, but you're still focusing on defense. Take the initiative." Liu pushed her back with a forceful shove.

Kai took a deep breath, forcing her anger down. She shifted her position, her eyes searching for an opening. Liu was right. She was too reactive, too cautious. She needed to take control, to direct the pace of the fight. Feigning a strike to Liu's left, he moved to block her, but she shifted her weight, bringing her blade around in a sweeping arc toward his right. Liu's eyes widened slightly in surprise, but he recovered quickly, parrying the blow.

"You're learning well," he said with approval.

Kai didn't let the compliment distract her. She pressed the attack, her strikes coming faster, more aggressively. Liu's blade met each one, but Kai could see she was pushing him now, forcing him to adjust.

They moved across the courtyard, their swords flashing, the clang of metal resonating off the temple. Kai could feel the strain in her muscles, the burn of exertion, but she pushed through it, driven by the desire to prove herself.

Liu's expression remained unreadable, but there was something in his eyes—pride, perhaps, or respect. It was hard to tell, but it gave her the strength to keep going, to push herself even harder.

Finally, Liu stepped back, lowering his blade. Kai hesitated, her chest heaving with exertion, but she lowered her blade as well, sensing the sparring session had come to an end.

"You're improving," Liu said. "But remember, Drakka are formidable enemies, and strength alone won't win you battles. They will outmatch you every time. You need to outsmart and outmaneuver your opponent. Above all, trust your instincts."

Kai nodded, wiping the sweat from her brow with the back of her right hand. She knew he was right. There was still so much to learn, but each session with him brought her closer to mastering the skills she needed to be Sworn. With Liu teaching her to fight, and Kokoro guiding her in the strengthening of her bond, she knew she would be ready when the time came.

Sensing a shift in the air, Kai turned to see Kokoro. She walked with measured steps and joined them. Liu bowed his head in respect and stepped away. Although Kokoro took the form of a human, Kai couldn't deny her presence was undeniably draconic, and the power she radiated was palpable.

"I see your improvement with each day," she said, nodding at Kai's sword.

"This is easy to navigate," Kai replied. "The bond less so."

"The bond is like a muscle. The more you exercise it, the stronger it becomes. Have you heard her voice yet?"

"No, but I've felt something. Emotions that aren't mine, but they're fleeting. I haven't been able to truly hear her thoughts."

"That is the beginning," Kokoro said, her tone reassuring. "The bond is still fresh, but you have already progressed further than I expected. It won't be long now before she speaks to you. Go bathe yourself and meet me here when you are done."

Kai sheathed her blade and bowed her head, then entered the temple and went to the bathing chamber. The warm water cleansed her body, but her mind was consumed with thoughts of her dragon. If Kokoro was right, she would hear her dragon's voice any day now. Still, doubts lingered. After spending her entire life not hearing the dragon that had originally chosen her, it was hard to believe that her experience now would be any different.

She emerged from the bath feeling refreshed. After drying and clothing herself, she returned to the courtyard where Kokoro waited. Kai's dragon was there, too, and her golden scales shimmered in the sunlight. With each breath, puffs of steam escaped her nostrils, curling and dissipating into the morning air.

"Today we are going to try something different," Kokoro said. "Close your eyes."

Kai obeyed, and she traced her fingers along the material of her pants, searching for a seam to run under her nails.

"Stop that," Kokoro said. "Quiet your mind and focus on your connection to your dragon. Do not force it. Let it come to you naturally."

Kai inhaled a deep breath and pushed all her thoughts aside. She imagined her bond as a thread of light, gold like her dragon's scales. It pulsed with life and energy. For a long moment, there was nothing but silence.

Then, she felt it—a gentle nudge at the edge of her consciousness, like a whisper carried on the wind. It was faint, almost imperceptible, but it was there. Kai's heart quickened as her dragon chirruped, but she forced herself to stay calm.

There was no voice, but there was a presence. A feeling washed over her, more powerful than any spoken language. Kai's breath caught in her throat. She'd not felt her dragon's spirit so clearly before. It was as though a door had been opened between them, allowing them to step into a place where their thoughts could meet.

Kai reached out hesitantly. The response came almost immediately, a wave of warmth that filled her with a sense of peace. She felt the true essence of her dragon; noble, fierce, strong. A rush of raw emotions flooded her mind: pride, love, determination, all amplified by the bond. It was overwhelming, but it was also beautiful. An unspoken word came to her, and she slowly opened her eyes to see Kokoro watching her intently.

"My dragon's name is Hikari."

CHAPTER TWO

Hikari.

It meant light, which Kai found fitting considering how her scales seemed to glow.

"A beautiful name," Kokoro said, glancing at the dragon. "Your connection is growing stronger, but it is still a fragile thing. To forge it into something unbreakable, you must face trials that challenge each of you, both physically and mentally."

"What sort of challenges?"

Kokoro's eyes turned skyward for a moment before settling back on Kai. "The skies are the domain of dragons. To truly understand Hikari, to trust in your bond, you must take to the air together. You must learn to fly as one."

The words sent a jolt of fear through Kai's chest. Flying, something she had always admired from the ground, was frightening. She had flown on the back of Siran's dragon to come to the temple, but that was a dragon with years of experience riding the skies. Hikari was practically a hatchling.

"I sense your fear," Kokoro said. "It is a natural response for humans, but it is one you must master."

"What if I can't... what if I fall?"

"You are not alone in this. Hikari will be with you. You will need to trust in her just as she will need to trust in you."

Kai felt a steadying presence wrap around her mind. Hikari's confidence flowed into her, pushing the fear aside. Kai nodded, inhaling a deep breath.

"I will guide you through this," Kokoro said.

Hikari lowered her massive body to the ground to allow Kai to climb onto her back. With trembling hands, Kai approached, running her fingers over the dragon's smooth scales. She could feel the dragon's strength beneath her touch, a living, breathing force of nature that she was now linked to. Kai hoisted herself onto Hikari's back and settled into place at the base of her neck, just ahead of her shoulders.

The fear was still present, but it was overshadowed by Hikari's confidence. The dragon spread her wings wide, their span casting shadows on the cobblestones. With a powerful beat, she lifted off the ground, and Kai watched the earth fall away from her. For a brief moment, panic made her stomach twist, but it was quickly smothered by the exhilaration that surged through her as they soared higher into the sky.

The wind whipped, tugging at her clothes and hair, but she barely noticed. Her entire being was focused on the sensation of flight—the rhythm of Hikari's wings, the rise and fall of their movements, the way the world below grew smaller and smaller until it was nothing but a patchwork of green and brown.

Kai's heart raced, but not from fear. The sky stretched out before them, an open expanse of possibility, and for the first time, she felt a sense of freedom she had never experienced before. She couldn't help but laugh. Focusing her thoughts on the bond, she sent words through it.

This is amazing. I never thought I could feel like this.

The bond hummed with harmony, and Kai knew that Hikari shared her feelings.

The world around them blurred as they entered the clouds, but they parted to reveal the vast blue above. Tears pricked at Kai's eyes, both from the sting of the cold and the pure, unfiltered emotions she felt. This was what it meant to be bonded to a dragon, to share not only thoughts and feelings, but experiences, to face the unknown together.

An unfamiliar voice touched Kai's mind, but she soon realized it was Kokoro.

It is easy to fly in clear skies, but you must be prepared for the worst. Look southeast, toward the mountains.

Kai turned her head, and her eyes widened. Dark clouds swirled ominously, and lightning flickered within them, casting brief, jagged illuminations across the mountain peaks.

I see a storm, Kai said.

The bond is tempered with adversity. Fly through the storm.

The thought of flying into such dangerous conditions brought her forgotten fear back to the surface.

But we've only just flown together for the first time. What if...

What if you succeed? What if you learn to trust in your bond even when the world around you is in chaos? This is not about mastering flight in calm skies. This is about learning to trust one another.

Kai swallowed hard, her throat dry. She knew she needed to strengthen the bond, but flying into a storm seemed a treacherous way to do so. Hikari's presence filled her mind again, calming her.

You are right, she told Hikari. *We can do this.*

Hikari circled around and headed directly for the storm. The air grew cooler as they approached the dark clouds, and the first gusts of wind hit them like a wall. Hikari's wings strained against the turbulence, and Kai could feel the tension in the dragon's muscles. She let out a mighty roar, fighting to keep herself on course as the wind threatened to throw them sideways.

The scent of rain and ozone was sharp in Kai's nostrils. Lightning flashed around them, followed by the deafening crack of thunder. Kai tightened her grip around Hikari's neck, but it was too thick for her arms to fully encircle. She closed her eyes and reached through the bond with her mind, trying to feel what Hikari was feeling—the currents of the wind, the shift of the air pressure, the instinctive adjustments the dragon made to stay aloft. Slowly, she began to sync with Hikari's rhythm, letting the dragon's instincts guide them through the storm.

They dodged several lightning strikes as Hikari banked sharply to avoid the dangerous currents that could send them spiraling out of control. Kai was still afraid, but the emotion was muted by her growing trust in Hikari. She could feel the dragon's confidence, her strength, and it bolstered her own. Feeling brave, she opened her eyes.

Suddenly, a powerful gust of wind caught them from below, lifting them higher than Kai had expected. For a terrifying moment, she felt weightless, the sensation of falling upward sending a jolt of panic through her. Before she could fully process what was happening, Hikari tucked her wings in and plunged downward, cutting through the wind like a blade. The speed was breathtaking, the air rushing past them in a roar. Kai's heart hammered in her chest, but she held on, trusting completely in Hikari's judgement.

The dive took them out of the worst of the storm and into a pocket of calmer air. Hikari flared her wings, slowing their descent just as another bolt of lightning streaked across the sky, narrowly missing them. Kai gasped, temporarily blinded from the flash of light.

After what felt like an eternity, the storm began to break. The clouds thinned, and the rain lessened, revealing patches of clear sky. Hikari's wing beats grew steadier, the turbulence easing as they left the worst of the storm behind. Kai could hardly believe they'd survived.

We did it, she said through the bond, feeling a deep sense of accomplishment. Hikari gave a triumphant roar in reply. As they flew back toward the temple, the sun peeked out from the clouds, casting a golden light over the mountains. The experience had changed something within Kai. She could feel it, a tangible difference in the bond. It was stronger, their connection more intimate.

When they landed in the courtyard, Kai slid off Hikari's back, her legs shaky. Kokoro smiled at her.

"You faced the storm and came out stronger for it. This is the essence of the bond between rider and dragon. It is not without fear, but it is through facing that fear together that you find true strength."

Kai bowed her head. "I understand now. It wasn't just about flying, it was about trusting Hikari, even when it seemed impossible. Forgive me for questioning you."

Kokoro laid a hand on Kai's shoulder, her touch warm. "There is no need to apologize. You are learning, and to learn, one must ask questions."

Hikari nuzzled Kai, and a wave of affection passed between them.

"Get something to eat and take a moment to recuperate. Your next trial awaits."

CHAPTER THREE

"You must seek out an artifact from ancient times. It is imbued with magic that has long since faded from this world. It is known as the Heart of Flame, and it rests in the heart of fire itself."

Kokoro's words echoed in Kai's mind as she sat upon Hikari's back, watching the landscape pass below. Trees and winding rivers slowly gave way to rugged terrain as they approached a mountain with its peak shrouded in a veil of smoke.

A volcano.

Hikari descended, landing at the base of the mountain where the earth radiated warmth, a harbinger of the inferno that awaited them within. A cavernous maw was open to the world, a passage carved into the mountainside by powerful forces, though whether natural or magical, Kai didn't know.

She dismounted and glanced around. The place was so foreboding, she doubted even the Drakka dared to tread here. The opening was wide enough even for Hikari's girth, and Kai was thankful she wouldn't have to brave the dangers of the cave alone.

"Are you ready?" she asked, running a hand along Hikari's scales.

In response, the dragon stared at her with a knowing gaze, then walked into the darkness. Kai cast a final glance at the sky and followed after Hikari. The air inside the cave was heavy and sulfurous, and Kai's lungs protested the oppressive heat that enveloped her. Hikari's massive silhouette was a reassuring presence against the gloom.

The cavern seemed to pulse with the heartbeat of the earth, a rhythmic thudding that matched her own racing heart. Each step took them deeper into the bowels of the volcano, and since Kai was blind in the dark, she was forced to rely on Hikari to guide her. She held onto the tip of her tail, stepping slowly and cautiously lest she slip on some unseen rock.

Beads of sweat formed on her brow, trickling down her temples, and her clothes clung to her skin. The heat was sapping her strength and clouding her focus. Kai stopped to rest and leaned against the wall. Hikari halted, and a wave of strength flowed through the bond, reinvigorating Kai.

She sent her appreciation to the dragon. There was no need for words; their bond transcended language. Pushing off the wall, she grabbed hold of Hikari's tail again and the two continued ahead. Kai wondered if the riders of old had faced similar challenges. Images flashed in her mind, but they weren't quite memories. The scenes were disjointed and confusing, but Kai was able to discern what Hikari was sending her were echoes of the past, moments lost in time that answered her question.

Yes, the riders of old had faced challenges, but ones much more difficult than she faced now. It was hard to take comfort in that when she felt as though she were suffocating.

A tremor ran through the earth beneath her boots, a murmur from the depths that set her heart racing. Somehow, she could discern the warning: the chamber they sought might soon become their grave. With the urgency of the mountain's message pulsing through her veins, Kai urged Hikari to quicken her pace.

The cavern around them slowly expanded, and the path coiled like a serpent, abruptly ending at an enormous pool of molten rock. The heat was far more intense here, and the air was so acrid it stung Kai's nostrils and made her eyes water. She blinked the tears away and noticed a trail of exposed stones that jutted up from the magma. On the other side of the pool, a luminous beacon flared in the shadows, revealing the entrance to a secondary chamber.

Kai had no doubts the beacon was the relic. Its magic called to her, a beckoning siren song that promised both glory and ruin. Hikari leaped into the air and spread her wings, gliding across the pool and landing on the other side. It was obvious the dragon expected her to navigate across on her own.

The relentless heat tested the limits of her endurance, but she forced herself to press on. She jumped onto the first stone, waving her arms wildly to help her stay balanced. The other stones were spaced closer together, and she nimbly moved across them. Every movement was a dance with danger, but she crossed the magma without incident. By the time she was safely on the other side, her breaths came in sharp gasps, the air searing her lungs as if it conspired with the molten rock to burn away her resolve.

Sweat dripped freely down her face and in places she never imagined possible, but she'd made it, and the chamber was just ahead. An aura of heat intensified with every step until she had to stop and fall back.

"I can't," she hissed. "It's too much."

Hikari sent images through the bond. They flashed vividly in Kai's mind, but they didn't make any sense to her. She wanted nothing more than to lie down and rest. Hikari growled and more images came to her mind.

"I don't understand…"

The dragon turned her gaze directly on Kai, their eyes locking. Another image came to her, and understanding dawned on Kai. She closed her eyes and focused on the bond. The single golden thread was crafted of many smaller threads, all woven together. Kai found the one in the image Hikari had showed her, and she touched it with her mind.

A magical shield spiraled into existence around her, a cocoon spun from the threads of their intertwined spirits. The barrier shimmered faintly with blue light, repelling the heat. Kai was still sweaty, but at least now she could breathe.

"Thank you. I owe you my life."

Hikari snorted and shook her head. Kai smiled, then looked at the entrance of the chamber. Together, they stepped inside. In the center of the space was a pedestal hewn from the rock, and lying atop it was an object that bathed the entire chamber in a crimson hue. It was a gemstone the size of Kai's fist, and the pulsing she felt in the air was coming from it.

Tentatively, Kai approached and extended a hand toward the relic. The moment her fingertips grazed its sparkling surface, her protective barrier winked out of existence, but instead of feeling the heat return, nothing changed.

The chamber began to tremble, and cracks spiderwebbed across the stone walls. It was as though the mountain rumbled at the disturbance of its treasure. Dust and small stones cascaded from the ceiling, and Kai sensed the earth was warning her to flee.

"Run!"

Turning on her heels, she sprinted out of the chamber, deftly crossing the pool of magma. She reached the other side and continued through the tunnel, the gemstone lighting the way. Hikari was right behind her, the dragon's footfalls echoing like thunderclaps in the hollow cavern.

The path turned treacherous as molten rock oozed from fissures that opened, a glowing menace that hissed and popped. Kai weaved between the obstacles, her agility tested by the earth's convulsions.

Her muscles screamed, yet she dared not slow her pace. Each stride took her closer to safety and away from the destructive embrace of the mountain that sought to reclaim its treasure. The ground heaved beneath her, and the sound of stone cracking reverberated throughout the corridor.

With a deafening crash, the path behind her gave way, succumbing to the mountain's wrath. A torrent of rocks and dust billowed into the air as Kai reached the threshold of the volcano's maw. She stumbled forward, propelled by the force of the eruption and Hikari's bulk. Her boots found solace on the firm soil beyond the reach of the inferno, and she turned back to see the passage was now a smoldering crater. The path was no more, entombed beneath layers of rock and dirt.

"Are you all right?" Kai asked, looking over Hikari with concern. Their bond burned fiercely, and her eyes widened when Hikari replied.

I am now.

CHAPTER FOUR

High above the clouds, the air was crisp and the horizon stretched endlessly. Kai enjoyed the cooler temperature, thankful that she and Hikari had escaped the volcano unscathed. She had tucked the Heart of Flame protectively inside the silk bag Kokoro had given her, and it rested firmly between her thighs while her hands gripped the scales of Hikari's neck.

The dragon's golden scales reflected the sun's light, casting a faint rainbow of color onto the surrounding clouds. When Kai was younger, she had often wondered what riding on the back of a dragon would feel like. It was better than anything she had imagined, but hearing Hikari's voice was the ultimate reward.

How were you able to show me those images? Are they memories?

I think they are, Hikari replied.

What do you mean? You don't know for certain?

No. They came to me by instinct, and I funneled them to you. I think they are memories from other elders.

Kai found that intriguing. How would a dragon receive memories from another, especially ones that were no longer around? She had many questions, but she feared she would overwhelm Hikari if she let them pour out unchecked.

As our bond strengthens, so do I, the dragon said, answering the main question burning in Kai's mind.

You can read my thoughts?

I can.

That made Kai a little uneasy. Did that mean she would never have privacy within her own mind?

I will not do it any longer without your permission, but you will need to learn to shield your mind from our bond.

Like you, I am still learning, Kai replied.

The wind changed direction, and the smell of smoke was overpowering. Kai leaned to the left, looking down at the ground below.

I smell it, too, Hikari said. *I hear screams.*

Can you reach Kokoro?

There was a moment of silence before Hikari answered, *No. I don't know how to link to her mind.*

Kai could faintly make out a village near the Tangsho river. Smoke billowed into the air, and she knew something was amiss.

We have to help them, Kai said. *Can you take me down there?*

The bond flooded with a mix of concern and pride. Kai thought Hikari would refuse, but the dragon responded with a surge of acceleration and dove, descending toward the village with the swiftness of an arrow. As they got closer, Kai could see the extent of the damage.

Thatched roofs succumbed to hungry flames. The roar of the fire mingled with the cries of the terrified villagers who were running in all directions. Hikari landed on the outskirts of the village, and Kai slid off her back, immediately running to the closest group of people.

"What happened here?"

A woman turned to face her, soot and tears streaking her face. "Drakka," she said. "They came out of nowhere."

Kai glanced around, suddenly afraid. She returned to Hikari and tied the silk bag around the dragon's neck, then drew her ebony blade.

"Go south," Kai instructed the villagers. "Cross the river and turn southwest to Tatenagawa. You'll be safe at the temple."

The small group fled past them, and Kai turned her attention to the village.

Keep watch for the Drakka, she told Hikari. *I'll get the other villagers.*

Without waiting for an answer, Kai hurried across the field and into the village proper. The heat from the flames was intense and threatened to singe her skin. She shouted for people to follow her, directing them toward the river. The acrid smoke filled her nostrils and stung her eyes, but she pressed on, determined to save as many as she could.

As she came around a bend, Kai froze. Several bodies lay in the dirt, but they hadn't been killed from the fire. Blood stained the earth beneath them, and judging by the footprints, they had been victims of a Drakka. Tightening her grip on the hilt of her blade, she cautiously continued ahead.

Sensing movement to her left, she whirled around, bringing her blade up and taking a defensive stance. Through the haze of smoke, a young boy appeared, coughing and gasping for air. His eyes widened at the sight of Kai's sword, but she held out a reassuring hand.

"I'm here to help. Come with me."

The boy accepted her offer and clung to her arm. She led him back the way she'd came, but a Drakka emerged from behind a partially collapsed building. It was similar in appearance to the one she'd seen at Ikje, but this one had red skin.

"Fire," she muttered to herself, realizing what had caused the flames. The Drakka spotted her, and a sinister grin spread across its face. Kai pushed the boy behind her and braced herself, focusing on the rhythm of her breathing. She'd sparred with Liu many times over the last few days, and although she had learned much, she knew she was not prepared to face a Drakka on her own.

The creature lunged at her, claws outstretched, but Kai deftly slapped its arm aside with her blade. The Drakka howled in pain and clutched its arm. Tendrils of smoke drifted off its flesh where her blade had touched it. She hadn't seen it do that before, but she only trained with Liu.

Your sword was forged to destroy Drakka, Hikari said. *I can sense the magic imbued within its metal. It hungers for their blood.*

Emboldened by her dragon's words, she attacked. Her blade struck true and cut a jagged zig-zag up the Drakka's forearm. Black blood oozed from the wound. The creature screeched in anger and struck Kai with its fist. The blow knocked her off her feet, sending her tumbling along the debris-strewn path. Kai landed hard and gasped for breath as pain shot through her side.

Get up, Hikari urged.

Kai struggled to her feet, her only concern for the boy who stood defenseless as the Drakka approached him. She felt her *ki* flare, pulsing in her veins like a drumbeat. Guided by intuition, she dug her fingers into the dirt and funneled the power she felt into the earth. The ground between the boy and the Drakka heaved upward, soil and stone rising to form a wall that intercepted the beast.

Kai's amazement didn't last long as the Drakka roared and pummeled the earthen barrier. It held, but Kai wasn't sure how long it would remain. She could feel her strength quickly fading and suspected the barrier was powered by her *ki*. With its attention diverted, the Drakka didn't see Kai until it was too late. She plunged her blade into its back, jerked it sharply, then yanked it free.

The Drakka let out a guttural scream that echoed throughout the village, its eyes widening in disbelief as it staggered briefly and fell to its knees. Blood spurted from the wound, and the creature fell face-first onto the ground, dead. Kai gasped as a sharp pain lanced through her ribcage, and the earthen barrier crumbled.

"To the river, hurry," Kai urged the boy. He nodded, wide-eyed, and ran off. The world around Kai spun and she dropped her sword.

I don't feel so good.

The last thing she saw was the ground coming up to meet her.

CHAPTER FIVE

When Kai opened her eyes, she found herself in an unfamiliar place. She struggled to make sense of the scattered images that flashed through her mind, and Hikari's own barrage of memories only added to her disorientation.

What happened?

You lost consciousness, Hikari replied.

Kai propped herself up on her elbows. She was lying on a straw mat in a large open hut. Several injured people were lying on similar bedrolls, and the room was filled with hushed groans and whispered prayers. The smell of blood and smoke was thick in the air, and the iron tang stung Kai's nostrils.

Where am I?

We're still in the village. After you collapsed, a group of warriors arrived and drove the Drakka away.

Are they still here? Kai asked.

Yes. They put out the fires and are helping to salvage what remains.

Kai forced herself onto her feet and stepped out of the hut. Her senses sharpened as she took in the chaos of what remained of the village. Homes were reduced to rubble and the earth was scorched, yet despite that, Kai could sense the resilience of the villagers. Some of them were already at work clearing the debris.

A group of individuals stood near Hikari, and Kai could tell by their bearing they were the warriors the dragon spoke of. Kai approached, and one of them turned to face her.

"You're awake. I feared the Drakka's fury had claimed you."

His voice, though soft, cut through the air with a clarity that commanded attention. His gaze locked onto hers, piercing in its appraisal.

"My name is Ryn. This is your dragon?"

"Yes," Kai answered.

"She is unique. I've never seen one quite like her before. What's your name?"

"Kai."

"You don't talk much, do you?"

"Only when it's necessary. Thank you for helping me. My dragon is still learning, and I don't think she would have known what to do for me."

Ryn's brows scrunched, but he said nothing.

"What brought you here?" Kai asked. "Your timing couldn't have been better."

"We've been tracking this group of Drakka for days. I wanted to catch them before they came across any settlements, but..." he glanced around at the village and sighed. "We weren't quick enough."

"I am sure the people here appreciate your efforts regardless. You said you were tracking the Drakka... where are your dragons?"

A pained expression briefly creased the man's face. "Our dragons are no longer with us."

Kai had heard of the Sundered before. They were Sworn whose dragons had died, usually at the hands of the Drakka. Instead of returning to a normal life, they devoted themselves to fighting the creatures on their own. She offered a silent nod of understanding. While she had only been bonded to Hikari for a short time, she knew that to lose that connection was to lose a part of oneself.

"How were you able to track the beasts? They hide their movements with magic."

"Ever since I was young, I've been able to sense the Drakka's stirrings. I thought it was something I gained through my bond, but the ability remains even though my dragon is no more."

"It seems like the emperor would put that to good use," Kai said.

"He probably would if I allowed him to. When my dragon died, I severed all ties to the empire. My brethren and I forge our own path."

Kai admired his resolve, though she wondered why he didn't see the value of using his talent alongside the Sworn.

"Where is the rest of your contingent?"

Kai debated on how to answer him, and before she could speak, he said, "You are welcome to join us. You are not Sundered like us, but we're on a quest and could use your help, and that of your dragon."

"I have my own duties to attend to," she replied. "But I am curious. Why would you need our help?"

"We have a way to deal a powerful blow to the Drakka, but we are not equipped to do it on our own. That is where you and your dragon would help."

Kai wished Kokoro was with them. She trusted the elder dragon's guidance, but she knew, too, that she would not always be able to rely on her. "What is your plan?"

"The Drakka employ underground caves to hide their eggs. I have found the entrance to one. If we can get inside, we can destroy the nest."

Kai's eyes widened in surprise. The idea of destroying a Drakka nest filled her with both trepidation and excitement. Being underground to retrieve the Heart of Flame was harrowing enough, but traveling into the earth and being surrounded by Drakka was another matter entirely. It wasn't ideal, but it was a worthwhile cause if it was successful.

"Why do you need my help? You seem to have enough men for such a task."

Ryn smiled at her. "Nothing can destroy Drakka eggs except dragon fire. You should know this."

Is that true? Kai asked Hikari.

It feels true. Although they are corrupted, they are a form of dragon.

"Why not go to the Sworn? They would relish the chance to strike at the Drakka."

"I told you already. I do not align with the empire." There was something in his tone that gave Kai the impression there was more to his story than the loss of his dragon, but if he had grievances with the empire, that was his concern.

How do you feel about this? I think we should consult with Kokoro.

Hikari regarded her intently, and Kai could see her reflection in the dragon's blue eyes. *I will follow your lead in this matter. If you want Kokoro's blessing, then we shall get it... but if you want to make your own decision...*

Kai didn't need to hear Hikari finish her sentence to know the dragon would follow her regardless of the outcome.

"What assurances do we have that this will work?"

"Assurances?" Ryn scoffed. "There are no assurances in war, but with my ability, we will be one step ahead of the Drakka if they sense our presence."

Kai considered the risks. "The bond we share with our dragons is..." she paused, searching for the right words. "Deeply woven. To have those threads torn from you... it is a wrong that cries out to be righted." She looked at Hikari, who lowered her head approvingly.

"We will help you."

CHAPTER SIX

As Kai stared into the black abyss, she questioned whether she had made the right decision. Hikari walked behind her, which offered some comfort, but the idea of being trapped belowground with Drakka made her heart quicken.

It had surprised her to learn the entrance to the nest was only a few hours march from the village, but in retrospect, she suspected that was probably where the attackers had originated from.

The tunnel was wide, and the air was cool. If Kai didn't know any better, she would have no idea the tunnel led to a nest of Drakka eggs. There were no foul smells lingering in the air, and the silence was broken only by the echoes of their footsteps. Ryn and his men were ahead of her leading the way, weapons drawn and ready, while their torches cast flickering shadows that danced along the rough-hewn walls.

The further they progressed, the more Kai felt as though someone was watching her. It reminded her of the day before the storm hit Ikje.

Ikje.

She prayed that her parents were safe, and that Master Satoshi had successfully repelled the Drakka attack. The more she thought about her parents, the more homesick she grew.

I would like to meet your parents, Hikari said.

Reading my mind again?

Guilt from the dragon washed over her.

It's all right, Kai soothed. *It is odd sharing my thoughts with another, but it's also nice to have someone to share them with. I never...*

Memories of her childhood came unbidden, flowing through the bond. She was alone. There was no one to talk with, and other children were forbidden from playing with her. The emptiness she felt stung her even now, and her eyes welled with tears. She blinked them away.

You are not alone any longer.

Hikari's words comforted her like nothing else.

Thank you for bonding with me, Kai said.

Thank you for awakening me. I don't know how long I slept, but it was far too long.

As they continued their trek, Kai's thoughts turned back to the task at hand. The air grew heavy and warm, and a faint odor began to permeate the darkness. Ryn held up a hand, bringing everyone to a halt. He crouched down, briefly examining the ground, then rose back up and motioned for everyone to continue.

The tunnel branched in two different directions, and Ryn led them along the path to the right. After roughly fifty feet, the tunnel opened into an enormous chamber. Along the top of the cavern, moss gave off an eerie fluorescent green glow, illuminating hundreds of dark eggs that lay nestled in earthen cradles. Kai froze as she took in the sight.

"There are so many," she said.

"And this is only one of their nests," Ryn replied. "Once your dragon burns the shells, we need to drive our swords into what remains to ensure they are truly dead."

Kai nodded and looked at Hikari. The dragon rumbled, the sound echoing in the vast, hollow chamber that acted as a womb within the earth. She trudged forward and leaned her head down, expelling a torrent of flames on the nearest eggs. The heat washed over Kai, and she had to take a few steps back from the intensity. The fire faded, and the eggs smoldered, small tendrils of smoke rising into the air.

Ryn and his men set about driving their blades into the shells. Kai watched them as they worked. These were hardened men. There was no hesitation in their strikes, no mercy. As the Sundered moved from one mound to another, their armor whispered with their movements. Feeling useless, Kai walked over to inspect their work.

The shells were as dark as her sword, though it was hard for her to determine if that was their natural color or from Hikari's flames. The punctures from the swords oozed inky liquid, and in one of them, she saw the small face of a Drakka, its mouth opened in a silent cry.

Guilt washed over her, and she turned away from the gruesome sight. She knew what was at stake, understood what needed to be done, but to destroy life before it had a chance to begin was a grim task. She took a deep breath and steeled herself, then drew her sword and joined the Sundered.

Kai's fingers tightened around the hilt of her ebony blade in a steadfast grip. With deliberate steps, she advanced to the nearest clutch of eggs and paused. The moment stretched taut as she raised the blade, the metal catching the light of the moss above in a sinister gleam. Her resolve faltered, and her hand tremored.

We do what we must, Hikari told her. *We are the shield against the darkness, the sword against chaos. We are not killing innocent creatures.*

Emboldened by her dragon's words, she thrusted the sword forward. The impact of steel upon shell sent a resonant clang throughout the chamber, the sound magnified by the hollowness of the cave. Kai plunged her sword into another egg. Shards flew. One after another, the eggs fell to her black blade.

The air grew fouler as they worked. The ichor that leaked from the eggs smelled like dead animals, and Kai's nostrils flared as she stifled a cough. She forced herself to breathe through her mouth, but she didn't find it much better since she felt as though she could taste the stench.

"Hold!" Ryn shouted.

All sounds ceased, and Kai glanced at him to see why they had stopped. After a tense moment that seemed to last an eternity, he said, "Continue."

The metallic chorus resumed, and after several minutes, Kai paused to wipe the sweat from her brow. Her arms ached from the effort, and judging by how much of the cavern they hadn't covered yet, she estimated they weren't even halfway done yet.

"This is taking too long," she said aloud.

"Press on," Ryn urged. "We don't have much time."

"Are the Drakka coming?"

His lack of an answer was all she needed. Kai glanced around the chamber, looking for an exit, but the light of the moss only illuminated so much, and everything else remained hidden in the shadows.

Do you see another way out of here? she asked Hikari.

There was a pause, and the dragon replied. *There is not.*

"We need to leave while we can," she told Ryn. "If the Drakka corner us in here…"

Ryn yanked his sword from an egg and turned to her, a wild look in his eyes. He was consumed with bloodlust.

"If we die, then we die with honor," he snarled.

The other Sundered stopped and looked at him. Kai could tell they weren't all in agreement with his words.

"Your grief is my grief," one of the men said. "But hope has not fled from us. If the Drakka are drawing close, I want to fight them on our terms, not theirs. Kai is right. If they catch us in here, we will all die."

Ryn's intensity diminished, and when he spoke, his words were calmer. "I-I'm sorry. You are both right. I let my hatred for these creatures get the better of me. We have done what we can for now. Let us leave, and we can return to finish this later."

Kai was glad he could be reasoned with. She didn't want to leave the Sundered down here, but she also wasn't going to risk death to destroy a few more eggs. Ryn sheathed his blade and marched across the cavern, heading back the way they'd entered.

"Wait," one of the Sundered said. "There's something there, in the darkness."

"What is it?" Ryn asked.

"I'm not sure. You should look at it."

Ryn hesitated, but he turned around and walked over to where the man stood. He knelt and inspected where the man indicated.

"There's nothing—"

The man struck Ryn in the side of the head, knocking him to the ground.

"Have you lost your mind, Shuji? What are you doing?"

The man, Shuji, pressed the tip of his sword to Ryn's throat.

"No one is going anywhere until Kai gives me her dragon."

CHAPTER SEVEN

"Shuji, you fool! You can't bond with the dragon. She's already bound to Kai."

"I'm not the one that wants her," Shuji replied. "The Drakka do."

Kai stared in disbelief at him. She barely knew these men, but she would never have suspected any of them would side with their enemy.

"You would betray your oath?" Ryn spat.

"My oath died with my dragon." Shuji paused, glancing at the other Sundered before his gaze fell on Kai. "I'm sorry," he said. "The Drakka have power beyond imagining. Our fight is a lost cause, and I would rather live under their rule than die. Make your choice now."

"Or what?" Kai asked.

"Or I'll kill Ryn. His blood will be on your hands."

"If you kill him, you won't get far before Hikari flames you to death."

"I'll take my chances," Shuji said, pressing his sword down and nicking Ryn's neck. A trickle of blood ran down his flesh.

Kai's hand trembled on the hilt of her sword, her mind racing through the impossible decision before her. The tension among the other Sundered was almost palpable.

"Your life will not be worth living under the Drakka," Kai said. "They consume everything. You know this. They may let you live for a time, but they will eventually consume you as well."

"I have no choice. They have my family."

"We will help you free them," Ryn said.

For a moment, Kai thought Shuji would be swayed, but her hopes were dashed when he shook his head.

"Your words feel like silk, but they are nothing more than cobwebs in the wind. Now, choose."

Hikari sniffed the air, turning her head toward the tunnel. *They are coming.*

"Time is running out," Shuji taunted.

Kai took a step toward the traitor, and he pressed his blade deeper into Ryn's neck, forcing her to stop. "Let him go," she pleaded.

"Give me your dragon and I will."

"That will never happen."

"Then you will all die here and the Drakka will take her anyway."

As if his words had summoned them, Drakka began to pour into the chamber from the tunnel. Kai's eyes widened in fear, but it was quickly driven away by anger. It sparked within her, swelling into a roaring inferno. With a defiant cry, she tapped into the bond, pulling from a hidden wellspring of power. It surged forth like a tidal wave, a torrent of energy that filled her very veins, setting every fiber of her being ablaze.

Her sword reacted to the power; its edge hungry for the blood of the Drakka. It came alight with an ethereal glow, and Kai drove the blade into the ground. The air itself seemed to scream, charged with the raw energy that poured from her. It was as if the souls of the elders lent their strength to her, guiding her hand. An aura of black light enveloped her, and the chamber quaked. The Drakka halted, looking around in confusion.

"Let him go," Kai demanded, her voice echoing through the cavern.

Shuji's eyes darted between her and the Drakka. Kai could sense his internal battle, torn between his loyalty to Ryn and his desire to see his family safe. Finally, he lifted his sword from Ryn's throat, his eyes never leaving Kai's. The other Sundered seized his sword and pushed him toward the Drakka.

The creatures charged, their confusion replaced with fury. Shuji was cut down mercilessly, and Kai felt a pang of sadness at his death. He had fallen for their tricks and betrayed his own kind. That thought fueled her anger further, and she rushed forward to meet the Drakka, her sword slicing through the air. She severed the heads of those closest, and Hikari joined her, blasting a stream of flames into the Drakka's ranks.

Their screams echoed in the cave as they fell, but their fellows weren't swayed. They continued to stream in from the tunnel, their numbers unending. Emboldened by her display, Ryn and the other Sundered fell in beside her, hacking and slashing.

Despite their valiant stand, Kai knew the power coursing through her wouldn't last forever. She scanned the chamber, looking for a way out, or at least some way to stall for time. And then she saw it, a hidden passage half concealed by a rockslide.

"There," she shouted, pointing with her sword. "Move that way!"

The Sundered followed her direction, slowly turning their back to it and retreating.

Can you move those rocks? Kai asked Hikari.

I will not leave your side.

You must. It's our only way to escape.

The dragon snarled and released another wave of flames, then bounded away. Kai thrusted her sword into a Drakka and began walking backwards alongside the Sundered. With Hikari gone, the Drakka crowded in closer, threatening to encircle them. A rumble filled the chamber as the stones were moved, and then Hikari was at Kai's side again, swatting Drakka aside with her claws.

The way is clear.

"Everyone into the tunnel! Hikari and I will hold them off!"

The Sundered broke away and ran for the exit. Kai could feel the power she had tapped into rapidly dwindling. Once the men were safe, Kai urged her dragon to go next.

You first, Hikari said.

I have a plan, and I don't want you in the way of what's coming.

Hikari's concern was evident in the bond, but she relented and hurried into the tunnel. Kai turned and sprinted for the opening, sliding to a halt as she reached the threshold. She turned back to face the Drakka and drew in a deep breath, hoping that whatever was guiding her wasn't leading her astray.

She held her black blade out before her and closed her eyes, pooling the remaining energy into the obsidian stone in the pommel. The sounds of the approaching Drakka faded, and time seemed to stand still. Warmth radiated from the stone, growing hotter with each passing moment. Kai could feel the energy preparing to burst forth, and her skin prickled with anticipation.

A flash of light blinded Kai even though her eyes were closed, and she was thrown backwards as the last of her energy was released in a violent burst. As the light faded, she lay gasping in the tunnel, her strength gone. After a few moments, she sat up, but her vision swam, and she slumped against the wall. When the nausea passed, she looked into the cavern.

Tendrils of smoke rose from the stone floor. The Drakka were gone, their bodies reduced to ash. Kai took a shaky breath and rose to her feet. Her legs felt as though they were made of jelly, but they held her up. She had no idea how she had wielded such power, but it had saved them. The cost was great, and she didn't know if you would be able to do it again. She searched for the well of power, but it was gone, no trace of it remained.

Kai was startled from her reverie when she heard footsteps, but it was only Ryn. He stared at her like she was a strange creature he'd just stumbled upon, but he offered her his hand. She accepted it and he helped her up the tunnel.

How did I do that? she asked Hikari.

I could feel the elders of the past guiding you, but otherwise, I do not know. Perhaps Kokoro will have the answer.

They navigated their way through the passageway in silence, eventually stepping out into daylight. Kai sat on the ground and noticed the Sundered were staring at her.

"What is it?"

"You are the Blooded One," Ryn said. As one, they all lowered to their knees and bowed to her.

"What are you doing? Get up."

"We are swearing fealty to you, Kai. You are the one spoken of in the scrolls, and we will follow you against the Drakka."

CHAPTER EIGHT

Despite Kai's protests, the Sundered insisted on following her and Hikari to Tatenagawa. They shared a meal to replenish their strength, and after a brief rest, Kai stood and walked over to the dragon, running a hand along her scales.

"We shouldn't stay here long," Ryn said, coming over to join Kai. "The Drakka are regrouping. You and your dragon should go. We'll meet you at the temple."

"On foot? If the Drakka catch you—"

"They won't," Ryn promised. "We know this land better than those creatures ever will." He clasped her on the shoulder, his grip firm but not unkind. "What you did down there… I've never seen anything like it. I know you will turn the tides of this war."

Kai doubted that was true, but she didn't say it. If the man believed it, who was she to tell him otherwise?

"I will see you at Tatenagawa, then," she said.

Hikari crouched low, and Kai climbed onto her back. She offered a nod to Ryn, who bowed his head respectfully.

I'm ready, she told Hikari.

The dragon spread her wings and took off, climbing into the sky. Kai watched the Sundered grow smaller, then turned her gaze ahead. It was an odd feeling having others view her as some sort of savior. She had never sought attention or fame, nor did she want it now, but if Kokoro was right, then Kai *was* the one from the prophecy...

The wind whipped at Kai's hair, and she turned her thoughts to her parents. She missed them dearly. How did they feel that their other daughter had sided with the Drakka? Were they appalled? Did they blame themselves for the path her life had taken?

Kai envisioned her sister, which wasn't difficult. They were twins, and their features were so similar that when Kai had seen her, she thought she was seeing an apparition.

As the temple's sloped roof came into view, she could see smoke rising into the air.

Do you see that? Kai asked.

Yes.

Hikari picked up speed, cutting through the air so quickly that Kai could feel her grip on the dragon's scales loosening. The temple grounds were overrun when they landed. Hikari set down in the courtyard, and Kai leaped down from her back and drew her sword.

A dozen Drakka were trying to break through the temple doors, but Hikari dispatched them with a blaze of fire. Kai kicked their charred remains aside and pounded on the door.

"Kokoro! Are you all right?"

There was only silence, and Kai's heart raced as she considered the worst. The doors swung open, and Kokoro stepped out to meet her.

"You arrived just in time," the elder said. "With your help, we can drive them away."

"Have they attacked the temple before?"

"Never. They have become bold indeed if they think they will overrun these sacred grounds."

"Where is Liu?" Kai asked.

"Here," he answered, exiting the temple. He was wearing his armor and had his sword in his right hand.

"He wouldn't leave my side," Kokoro said. "As if I need a protector. Come, let us make these Drakka regret ever stepping foot here."

The three of them spread out in front of Hikari. Kai stood to Kokoro's left, and Liu stood to the elder's right. A group of Drakka came around the side of the temple and shouted battle cries, rushing toward them.

Kai and Liu charged ahead to meet them while Kokoro stayed close to Hikari. They were outnumbered by the Drakka, but they had the advantage of Hikari's flames. Liu and Kai met them head-on, their swords clashing against the Drakka's weapons.

Kai ducked under a sweeping blow, then thrust her black blade into the creature's midsection. The Drakka let out a roar before collapsing to the ground. She pulled her sword free and finished it off, then turned to the next attacker. She tried to parry a strike, but she was no match for the creature's brute strength, and she staggered back from the blow.

Liu came to her aid, his blade separating both of the Drakka's arms at the elbow. Dark blood spurted onto the cobblestones, and Liu swung his sword in an arc, removing its head. Its body toppled to the ground.

"Thank you," Kai said breathlessly. Liu nodded in reply, engaging another of the Drakka.

The two continued to cut through the Drakka's ranks, but Kai could feel her strength waning. It had been a long day, and exhaustion was setting in. She took a moment to glance at Kokoro.

"Use the heart," the elder urged.

"What do you mean?"

Kokoro's words were drowned out by the clash of steel, and Kai turned her attention back to the Drakka in time to see a clawed hand. It struck her in the head, and the next thing she knew, she was lying on the ground staring up at the sky.

She groaned as she sat up and forced herself back onto her feet. Liu was surrounded, and Kai cursed under her breath. She grabbed her sword off the ground and rushed forward, driving it into the back of the nearest Drakka. Wrenching the blade free, she thrust the tip of the blade into the neck of another.

Get down, Hikari warned Kai.

She looked at the dragon and could see the dragon's throat glowing with orange light.

"Down!" she shouted, tackling Liu to the ground. An intense heat washed over her as Hikari flamed the Drakka. Kai rolled around, fearing her clothes had caught fire, but she was unscathed. Hikari's precision was miraculous.

Impressive.

Thank you, Hikari replied, her pride filling the bond.

Kai helped Liu back up, then brushed ash from her clothes.

"That was a small force," Kokoro said. "I fear more will come. It is obvious to me that your sister is directing them."

Liu sheathed his blade. "Let them come. We will slay them all."

"Do not speak foolishly," Kokoro chastised him. "We are outnumbered, and there are no allies nearby."

"While Hikari and I were gone, we met a group of Sundered. They have pledged to help us against the Drakka. They are on their way here."

"How many do they number?"

"Only a handful, but they are skilled warriors."

"It is not enough," Kokoro said.

"You can transform into your true self. I am sure the Drakka would cower and flee at the sight."

Kokoro smiled sadly. "I suppose they would, but it is not possible. My spirit fades, and with it, my power. I hope to complete your training before..."

Kai frowned. "Before what? Do you mean you are dying?"

"Yes, I am dying. I have lived longer than any of my kind before me, and I am weary."

"But we need you," Kai said. "We cannot defeat the Drakka without you."

"You will be fine without me. I sensed a great power while you were gone. It was you, wasn't it?"

Kai nodded.

"Tell me what happened."

CHAPTER NINE

The setting sun cast long shadows across the courtyard as Kai recounted the events from her quest at the volcano. Kokoro listened intently, and her expression was grave as Kai finished.

"You showed great courage entering the nest of the Drakka, but your greatest trial lies ahead."

"What do you mean?" Kai asked.

"To defeat the Drakka is one thing, but to face your own kind is another. Can you strike down your own flesh and blood? Your sister?"

The question left Kai speechless. She stared at the elder in silence, her thoughts racing from one scenario to another.

"I cannot answer that. Not now, at least. It's not something I'd considered. I was hoping…"

"That you could save her somehow?" Kokoro smiled sadly. "It is a pleasant thought, but I do not see any hope for that. In the end, it will be you or her. Only one can prevail."

"It can't be that simple," Kai argued. "I know I don't know her, but it doesn't feel right."

"It is not simple," Kokoro replied. "But it is necessary. You should prepare yourself for what must be done. But enough of that. There is another matter we must discuss."

Kai was thankful for the change of subject. The thought of fighting her sister, let alone killing her, was hard to imagine. And yet, she knew what was at stake was much greater than any sibling loyalty. The fate of the empire hung in the balance.

"There is another item that will help you to defeat the Drakka. It has long been hidden from human eyes."

"What is it?" Kai asked.

"I had hoped to never speak of this relic, let alone see it used again. But desperate times call for desperate measures."

As Kokoro explained the nature of the item, Kai listened with a mixture of fear and awe. A cloak made from the hide of an elder dragon? The ability to move between what was visible and invisible? It seemed unbelievable, yet Kokoro had also told her of the Heart of Flame, and that was real.

"The shadow realm," Kai repeated, murmuring the words.

"It is a place where light and dark coexist, and time flows differently. It is a realm of great power and even greater danger. The cloak allows its wearer to traverse the boundaries between our world and the shadow realm, granting them abilities beyond mortal sight."

Kai ran her fingers along her leg. She found a seam and ran it under her nails. "If this artifact is so powerful, why has it been hidden away? Why has it not been used before?"

"Power always comes with a price. The cloak is as much a burden as it is a blessing. It has driven many to madness, consuming them with the allure of its abilities."

Kai's unease caused her voice to break when she asked, "And you think I can wield it without succumbing to its influence?"

"Your heart is pure, and your intentions noble... but make no mistake, using it will test you in ways you cannot yet imagine. With your dragon's strength behind you, I am confident you will not be swayed."

"I will do what is needed."

"Very good," Kokoro said. "Rest while you can. You will need to leave in the morning."

The elder took her leave, returning to the temple. Kai was tired, but there was too much on her mind. She found a bamboo bucket and began cleaning the remains of the Drakka from the courtyard. Considering they were piles of ash, it didn't take long for her to cleanse the grounds of the creatures. She washed the bucket out in the river, then filled it with water and scrubbed the cobblestones by hand. Kai could feel Liu's gaze on her as she worked.

"You have grown much in a short time," he said.

"It doesn't feel like it."

"That is because you are focused on where you are going, and not where you are or where you've been. When you only think about the future, you lose sight of the past."

Kai had to admit there was truth to his words, but she didn't say anything.

"You've become stronger, wiser, and more determined." He paused. "But there is one thing that I haven't seen change in you. Your compassion. It's what makes you different from other riders."

"It's not my intention to be different," Kai said, ceasing her scrubbing for a moment and looking up at him.

"Of course not. That's not what I was implying. I merely mean that you don't see the world the same as others. That's not a bad thing."

Kai smiled slightly, then continued her task. "Do you think Kokoro is right about me? That I can use the cloak?"

"That remains to be seen, but I believe in you."

Kai's cheeks flushed. When she'd first met him, she thought he was nothing more than a rough soldier who'd been assigned as her guard. The more she got to know him, the more she realized there was more to him than a sword and armor. He was her friend.

"Thank you," she said softly.

"For what?"

"Everything."

"I haven't done much besides teach you to wield a blade," he said, chuckling. "But you're welcome."

Once Kai felt the courtyard was properly cleaned, she returned to the river and washed the sweat and grime from herself. The cool water soothed her aching muscles, and she felt somewhat rejuvenated. Hikari laid on the grass nearby, and Kai felt vulnerable enough to remove her clothes and clean them. By the time she set them on the riverbank to dry, the sun was gone. Hikari used her breath to warm them, and after a few moments, the moisture had vanished.

Kai dried herself as best as she could, then put her clothes back on and laid on the grass beside Hikari, watching the stars twinkle into existence. She closed her eyes, feeling the weight of the day on her mind and body.

As she slept, she dreamed of battling the Drakka, of mastering the power of the cloak, and of facing her sister. When she awoke, the sun was beginning to rise. Kai sat up, startled she'd slept so long.

"Ah," she groaned, rubbing her stiff neck muscles. "Why did you let me fall asleep out here?"

I didn't want to disturb your rest, Hikari replied. *It was also nice to have some company, even if you weren't coherent.*

Kai got to her feet and stretched, then rubbed the sleep from her eyes. Her stomach growled, and she realized she hadn't eaten anything before falling asleep. She made her way to the temple and found Liu standing in the courtyard eating rice cakes. He offered her some, and she devoured several of them eagerly.

"You're not hungry, are you?" A smile tugged at his lips.

"I've never felt hungrier," Kai said, taking another rice cake from his plate and biting into it. "I don't think I moved the entire night."

"Using magic has that effect," Kokoro said as she joined them. "You must be careful not to push yourself too hard."

Kai finished chewing and wiped her mouth with the back of her hand. "Where is this cloak I need to find?"

Kokoro pointed north. "A crypt lies in Shaoing beyond the Shinraha Mountains. Spectral guardians protect it and will challenge you."

"What kind of challenges will they pose?"

"Tests of will, wisdom, and courage. You must pass them all to obtain the cloak. Liu, I want you to go with her. Hikari should be able to carry you both, and Kai will need your help."

Liu bowed his head respectfully.

"I have packed you some supplies for the journey. It will take you at least two days, for Hikari will not be able to fly the entire way without rest. Be wary. Shaoing was once protected by my brother, but he has been gone many years, and I am sure the Drakka have taken over his temple."

"We will be careful," Liu said, taking the pack of supplies from Kokoro. "And we will return as quickly as possible."

Kai was grateful for his confidence. The only thing running through her mind was one question.

Am I truly ready for this?

CHAPTER TEN

The sun cast a golden hue over the jagged peaks of the Shinraha Mountains. Their snow-capped summits gleamed, and a chill wind nipped at Kai's flesh. She kept her eyes on the horizon, the monotony of the landscape below broken by the occasional glimpse of wild game.

Liu was seated behind her, his hands resting on her waist. Under normal circumstances, it would have made her feel uncomfortable, but she knew he was merely holding onto her to keep from being pulled away by the wind. There was nothing more to his loose embrace, and she appreciated the warmth that radiated from him.

They had been flying for a few hours, and Kai could sense the fatigue in Hikari's wing beats. She patted the dragon on the neck comfortingly.

You should rest, she said.

Hikari snorted in response, sending tendrils of smoke into the air that quickly dissipated.

Land at the next clearing, Kai insisted.

A few moments later, Hikari descended to the base of the mountains. They landed with a soft thud, and Kai slid down the dragon's shoulder, her legs aching from the hours of riding. The wind howled between the peaks, the sound almost like distant voices.

"I'll build a fire," Liu offered.

As he set about collecting wood, Kai wrapped her arms around herself. The air was cold and thin, and it bit into her bones even through her clothes. She hoped Hikari wouldn't need long to rest. She hated the cold.

Liu placed several sticks in a pile and drew his sword, swiftly sliding a stone up and down the edge of the blade. A few sparks came to life, but it wasn't enough to ignite the wood.

"Watch out," Kai said.

Liu looked up just as Hikari huffed, expelling a small ball of flame that struck the pile and set the wood alight. He sheathed his sword and sat down, holding his hands out near the fire. Kai sat down opposite him and huddled as close to the flames as she dared. Hikari curled into a ball behind her and was soon asleep.

Kai watched the flames dance, lost in her thoughts. She thought of her sister again and wondered how life would have been had things gone differently. Would they have still shared a bond with the same dragon? Or would one of them have faded from the bond for the benefit of the other?

Perhaps it wouldn't have been her sitting here in the cold mountains on a quest to find an ancient crypt, but Akuhara instead. Kai looked up from the fire to see Liu staring at her.

He broke the silence, his voice soft but edged with curiosity. "Are you all right? You look upset."

"I'm just thinking."

"You're thinking about *her,* aren't you? Your sister?"

"Yes. It feels wrong to abandon any hope of saving her, but you heard Kokoro. She thinks there is no salvation for her."

"Things don't always unfold the way we wish they did," Liu said. "I know that doesn't help nor comfort you, but life is harsh. We must weather these things as best as we can without losing our humanity."

Hikari stirred in her sleep, and Kai glanced at her.

"Do you think dragons feel things like we do?"

Liu's brow furrowed as he considered the question. "I think they feel everything more deeply than we know. But they don't dwell on the past like we do. They live in the now, in the heart of the moment. Maybe that's something we can learn from them."

Kai contemplated his words. Maybe he was right. She couldn't control the events of the past, but she could sway events happening now. The wind howled again, louder this time, and Kai's gaze traveled to a rocky ridge. The sound was different—less like the wind and more like something alive.

Liu noticed it, too. His hand drifted to the hilt of his sword. "Did you hear that?"

Kai stood, her muscles tensing as she peered beyond Hikari's bulk. Her breath hitched when she saw them— hulking forms, their silhouettes unmistakable. They were trudging down from the mountains.

"Drakka," Kai hissed. "Put out the fire!"

Liu was already a step ahead of her, shoveling dirt with his hands and dumping it onto the flames.

"How many?" he asked.

"Too many."

"Have they seen us?"

Kai hesitated. "I don't think so."

They waited in silence and watched as the Drakka passed by their location. The creatures moved in a slow, methodical line, far different from their usual behavior. Kai counted at least twenty, their bodies rippling with unnatural strength.

When the last of them disappeared from view, Kai let out a sigh. "We got lucky. If they had seen us..."

Hikari lifted her head, sniffing at the air. *I smell Drakka nearby.*

They've passed through here already, Kai replied.

"Did you notice the direction they're heading in?" Liu asked.

Kai followed the path the Drakka took and realized they were traveling southwest. "Do you think they are going to Tatenagawa?"

He shrugged. "That's impossible to know, but Kokoro can take care of herself. We need to keep moving. If they catch our trail, we aren't in the best position to defend ourselves." Liu looked at Hikari. "Are you rested enough to continue?"

Hikari stretched her wings and yawned. Kai could feel the dragon's weariness had lessened, but her strength wasn't fully restored.

I can manage, Hikari said, projecting her thoughts for both of them to hear.

Are you sure? Kai asked.

Yes.

The sun was in the middle of the sky, but despite it being midday, the temperature seemed to be getting colder. Kai wanted to give Hikari more time to rest, but she also wanted to be gone from this place.

Let us get moving, then. We will stop again at nightfall unless you can't make it that far. There is no need to push yourself beyond your limits.

Hikari rumbled her agreement, and Kai and Liu climbed onto her back. The wind picked up as they took to the air, but Kai ignored the chill. They soared above the snowy peaks, and the air grew so cold Kai could see her breath puff out in small clouds.

They flew until they were beyond the bulk of the mountains. The air grew gradually warmer, and Kai pointed to a grove of trees.

We'll camp there for the night, Kai said. *It'll provide cover and we should be able to keep a fire going without worrying about prying eyes.*

Hikari took them down, landing just outside of the tree line. Liu and Kai went to work setting up camp while Hikari went hunting for food. They soon had a crackling fire going, and they shared a meal of fresh fruit and fish from the supplies Kokoro had given them.

The wind eased as night engulfed the land, and the stars shined above the tree canopy. Kai's belly was full, and she lounged beside the fire, her eyes heavy. She was surprised how tiring it was doing much of nothing.

"I'll take first watch while you get some sleep," Liu offered.

Kai laid her head down on her arms and closed her eyes, drifting off to sleep. Once again, strange dreams haunted her.

CHAPTER ELEVEN

Kai awoke to the chirping of birds. She blinked several times, confused at where she was. Slowly, her wits returned, and she stared at the charred wood and ash, all that remained of the fire from the night before.

She sat up and looked around, rubbing her eyes. Liu was asleep, but Hikari was awake, keeping a vigilant eye over them.

Did you find food? Kai asked.

I found a few deer, the dragon replied. *And I slept while Liu kept watch. He was going to wake you, but I couldn't sleep anymore, so I took over.*

Thank you. I needed that.

Kai rose to her feet and stretched. She'd slept longer than she expected, and she felt fully refreshed.

I scouted ahead last night. We aren't far from Shaoing.

How much further is it?

A few hours, Hikari replied.

Kai rummaged through the bag of food Kokoro had given them and settled on a rice cake wrapped in seaweed. She ate in silence and enjoyed the sights and sounds of the woods around her. Wandering away from the camp, she relieved herself among some bushes and found a small stream where she splashed ice-cold water on her face. She drank her fill and returned to the camp, gently shaking Liu until his eyes snapped open.

"Time to get moving," she said. "Hikari says we'll reach Shaoing today."

Liu grunted and got up, rubbing sleep from his eyes. He ate a rice cake and drank from the stream, then packed their meager belongings. They were gone soon after, cutting through the morning air on Hikari's back.

A few hours later, just as Hikari had said, Shaoing came into view. A monolithic structure of weathered stone stretched skyward, its crumbling walls marred by deep cracks and overgrown with twisted vines.

Hikari landed in front of the temple, a low growl rumbling in her chest. *This place is not natural. It has been shaped by something old... powerful.*

Kai dismounted and slid to the ground, her boots sinking into the damp earth. She could faintly sense what Hikari was talking about. There was something in the air, a humming of some kind, but when she tried to focus on where the sound was coming from, it changed direction on her.

Do you sense any Drakka? Kai asked.

Hikari sniffed the air and snorted, her nostrils flaring. *I only smell the stench of decay.*

Massive stones had collapsed over the entrance of the temple, leaving an opening too small for the dragon. As much as she didn't like the idea of leaving Hikari behind, the dragon would have to wait outside for them.

"Liu and I will go inside," she said aloud. "If something happens, I will let you know."

Hikari stepped forward and attempted to lift the stones out of the way, but they were too heavy even for her. She grumbled and retreated, admitting defeat.

We'll be back, Kai promised.

Together, she and Liu crawled on all fours through the opening and entered the darkness of the temple. Once they were past the boulders and across the threshold of the doorway, they were able to stand. Kai's eyes struggled to adjust to the gloom. Pale, phosphorescent lichen clung to the walls, casting a glow that did little to dispel the darkness.

"Stay close," Liu said, stepping in front of her. "We don't know what sort of traps might lurk in these halls."

They made their way forward slowly, and the narrow hall they were in opened into a large antechamber. The walls were bare, and the stone floor was littered with dirt and small rocks.

"This place feels like it's been abandoned for a long time," Kai whispered, her eyes darting around the room for any sign of the guardians Kokoro had warned her about.

As if summoned by her thoughts, a shadow detached from the wall. It was tall, cloaked in dark robes that blended in with the stones. The figure moved with an unnatural grace, its face hidden beneath a hood. Kai's hand tightened on the hilt of her sword, but it made no move to attack. It stopped several paces away and pulled its hood back, revealing a skeletal face marked with runes. Where its eyes should have been were golden orbs that burned with fire.

"Why do you tread here?"

Its voice caused a chill to crawl down Kai's back. She glanced at Liu, who kept his gaze on the figure, his sword partially unsheathed. Pushing her fear aside, Kai said, "I seek the cloak."

"You must prove yourself worthy," the guardian replied.

"How do I do that?"

"Face the trials. If you are worthy, you will be given the cloak. If you fail, you will die."

The guardian's last word echoed ominously off the walls. Kokoro had mentioned it would be dangerous, true, but she hadn't said anything about possibly dying. Kai swallowed hard.

"You don't have to do this," Liu said.

"I know," she replied.

Although she knew his words were true, she felt like she didn't have a choice. Kokoro hadn't steered her wrong yet, but the threat of death gave her pause. Kai thought of her parents, of the innocent people across the empire who suffered from the Drakka. If she could save even one life by risking her own, was it worth it? She thought it was.

"I accept," she said.

The guardian's orbs glowed brighter. "Very well. Hear my riddles and answer correctly to pass forth. I am not alive, but I grow; I don't have lungs, but I need air; I don't have a mouth, but water drowns me. What am I?"

Kai repeated the words within her mind. *Not alive... grows... needs air... water drowns it.* Her eyes widened with realization. "The answer is fire."

"Correct," the guardian said, a hint of approval in its ethereal features. "I am invisible, but I carry clouds; I am weightless, but I can move the strongest tree; I have no voice, but I make whispers and howls. What am I?"

"Wind," Kai answered, relieved the riddle was easy. She wondered how many of these she would need to answer.

"Correct. I am not alive, but I cradle life; I am patient, and I shape mountains with time; I wear no clothes, but flowers adorn me. What am I?"

"Any ideas?" Kai asked Liu.

"No!" the guardian hissed. "Only you may answer."

Kai considered the riddle for a moment, unsure of what could not be alive but could shape mountains. Her first guess was the wind, but that was the answer of the last question, and flowers didn't adorn the wind. She opened her mouth, then closed it, doubting herself. Finally, she decided on an answer. "The earth?"

"Correct." The guardian's skeletal face turned serious. "Here is your final riddle. I have no shape, but I can fill any form; I am silent, but I can also roar; I am gentle, but I can carve stone. What am I?"

Kai's mind was blank. She looked at Liu again, the panic on her face obvious. He couldn't give her the answer, but maybe he could provide some sort of clue.

"The other questions are all connected," Liu said. "What connects them?"

The guardian didn't object, so Kai assumed Liu's help was acceptable. She considered the other answers. Fire, wind, earth... they were all elements.

"Water," she answered.

"Correct. You have proven your wit. You may advance to the next chamber."

The guardian's form flickered briefly and then dissipated in a flash of light, scattering motes of dust.

"Thank you," Kai said. "That almost ended in disaster."

CHAPTER TWELVE

Upon exiting the chamber, they found themselves in a hallway. Kai expected another apparition to confront them. Instead, they found the corridor was empty. Strange symbols were carved into the walls, pulsing with an eerie glow. Kai reached out, her fingers hovering inches from a particularly intricate carving. It resembled a dragon's eye, and as she watched, the pupil dilated, focusing on her. She jerked her hand back.

"Did you see that?" she asked.

"See what?"

She stared at the symbol for a moment, waiting, but nothing happened. "Never mind. Maybe I'm seeing things."

They pressed on, navigating the winding passage. The symbols seemed to guide the way, glowing brighter as they approached intersections and dimming as they passed. Kai was lost in her thoughts, and Liu startled her when he suddenly stopped and grabbed onto her arm.

"Look."

Ahead, the hall opened into a vast chamber, this one bigger than the last, and its floor was covered with stone tiles. Some bore the same glowing symbols as the walls, while others remained dark.

"This feels too easy," Liu said. "I think it might be a trap."

Kai took a cautious step forward, placing her foot on a tile bearing the familiar dragon eye symbol. It glowed brighter beneath her weight, but nothing else happened.

"I think we need to follow the path of symbols. The dark tiles probably trigger something."

Liu nodded. "That makes sense. Do you want me to go first?"

"No, I'll go."

Kai took another careful step, her body tense, ready to react at the slightest sign of danger. With each successful step, her confidence grew, but so did the pressure. One mistake could mean the difference between reaching the cloak and failing not just herself, but everyone. The glowing markings emitted heat, and the room became oppressively hot. Sweat was beading on her brow by the time she neared the exit.

She hopped from the final tile to the threshold of an archway that led to a corridor with a dirt floor. Liu followed the path she had taken, and when he reached her side, they continued ahead side by side. A few steps in, the stone walls groaned and scraped as they twisted, sliding like immense puzzle pieces to form a labyrinth.

"I saw another door back there. Maybe we can—" Liu's words were cut off by a resounding thud as a stone slab fell behind them, blocking the doorway. There was no going back.

The labyrinth walls hummed with energy, and Kai rested a hand on one to see if she was supposed to use magic to direct the maze. The stone was cold and unyielding, but there was a strange vibration beneath its surface. A soft, rhythmic pulse, almost like—

Liu stepped past her, and the ground beneath her feet trembled. Kai pulled him backward. The walls shifted again, the stones grinding together as they formed a completely different path.

Kai frowned. "It changed." The walls that had been stationary moments ago had rearranged themselves as if they were alive.

"We need to move before it closes us in or crushes us," Liu said. He started forward again, but Kai hesitated.

He was right, but something about the way the walls moved—deliberate, methodical—didn't make sense. She looked down the corridor that had just opened in front of them, then to the side where another path had formed. The stones continued to grind and shift, but Kai wasn't listening to the sound of the walls. She was focused on the space between the noise, the stillness that came before each movement. There was a pattern. She could feel it, faint and elusive, but it was there.

"This place isn't just a maze," she said slowly. "It's testing us."

"What do you mean?"

"It's not about finding the right path. It's reacting to us, to how we move. We can't just charge through it."

"If we stand here, we're dead. Let's go this way." Liu strode to the left, but another tremor shook the floor, and the corridor sealed shut with a heavy slam. Kai's mind raced. The walls weren't moving randomly. They were trying to force them to make hasty decisions. It wanted them to panic. She didn't know how she knew that, she just... knew.

"Every time we move, it changes. But if we stand still..." Kai held Liu in place and gestured to the corridor in front them. It remained open, though the walls trembled slightly. "It waits."

Liu shook his head. "So what do we do? Stand here?"

"Not exactly," Kai answered, her voice firmer now. "We need to move when it lets us, not when we want to. It's like a dance."

Liu gave her a look of disbelief. "A dance with a shifting stone labyrinth that wants to crush us? Great."

"We just need to listen."

Kai closed her eyes, focusing on the subtle rhythm beneath her feet. It was like the beat of a drum. When the next shift came, she felt it in her bones.

"Now," she whispered, opening her eyes.

She stepped forward and Liu followed without hesitation. The walls stayed still for a moment longer, but as they walked, Kai could hear the low rumble of stone shifting behind them. Her heart pounded, her senses heightened. They turned a corner, and the ground trembled again, the path behind them closing off.

"Keep going," Liu urged.

"No. Wait."

Liu froze in place. Kai closed her eyes again, feeling for the pulse. The walls shifted, but only slightly. The path ahead remained open. She moved cautiously, pausing with every tremor in the stone. The labyrinth shifted around them, but now they were in sync with it, anticipating each change before it happened. The panic that had gripped Kai moments ago eased, replaced with a growing confidence.

Finally, they turned another corner and Kai saw it: a wide archway bathed in light. "That's it," she said. Liu started forward, but Kai held him back yet again. "It's not over yet."

"The exit is right there."

"I know, but it is still testing us. It wants us to rush."

The pressure in the air seemed to build as they stood there, the walls rumbling with impatience. Kai held her ground, waiting. She could feel the pulse, fainter now, but still there.

"Walk," she said. "Slowly."

Liu fell into step beside her. They moved toward the archway, and the walls groaned, but they didn't close in. As they reached the exit, the pressure lifted, and they stepped through. The labyrinth sealed shut behind them.

Liu looked at her. "Remind me never to question your instincts."

CHAPTER THIRTEEN

The archway opened into a vast, tranquil garden. The ceiling above was lost in twilight, dotted with soft stars, and the ground was a lush carpet of green grass.

Kai looked around, entranced by the beauty. A soft breeze drifted through the trees, carrying the scent of cinnamon and honey. Natural winding pathways stretched out in every direction, each one lined with flowers of a different color. Statues of robed figures stood at intervals along the paths, their expressions calm and inscrutable.

"It's peaceful here," Liu said. "Too peaceful."

Kai nodded, her muscles still tense from the labyrinth. "It looks like another maze, but I don't see any logic to this one."

As they moved deeper into the garden, the paths seemed to multiply, twisting and turning until it became impossible to tell which direction they'd come from. There was no clear indication of which path to take, and every turn seemed to lead to another set of branching trails.

Kai knelt beside one of the paths and touched the flowers. They were real, soft and fragrant. But as she stood, she realized something troubling—each path seemed more enticing than the last. One was lined with radiant golden flowers, glowing softly under the twilight sky. Another was shaded by towering trees, their leaves shimmering silver. In the distance, she could hear faint music, as though someone were playing a hauntingly familiar melody just out of sight.

"Do you hear that?" she asked.

Liu tilted his head. "Music. But... where is it coming from?"

Kai's heart skipped a beat as the melody became clearer. It wasn't just any music. It was the song her mother used to hum to her when she was a child, a melody long forgotten. She swallowed hard, her throat tightening.

"We need to be careful. This place is playing tricks on us."

Kokoro had said the trials would test her will, wisdom, and courage. What sort of test was this? Every path seemed to draw her in, each one more convincing with its temptations.

"How do we figure out which path leads to the next chamber?" Liu asked.

Kai shook her head. She considered the previous tests. The garden wasn't testing her endurance or strength. Perhaps it was testing her ability to discern, to choose wisely. But how could she make a wise decision when each path felt like the right one?

Her eyes drifted to a trail lined with glowing red flowers, their petals delicate but vibrant, almost pulsing with light. The temptation was there, tugging at her, urging her to follow it. But something about it felt... wrong.

"I don't think we're supposed to follow what we want," Kai said. "I think this garden is designed to lead us astray. The more we want something, the more dangerous it becomes."

Liu glanced down a path filled with silver leaves, his eyes narrowing in suspicion. "So we should ignore everything that looks good?"

Kai didn't answer right away. Her gaze wandered over the myriad paths, the winding trails, the intoxicating smells and sights. The music tugged at her heart, but she forced herself to listen beyond it. Somewhere in this garden, there had to be a path that was true, one that wasn't about indulgence or desire.

A statue caught her attention. It stood taller than the others, its stone face worn with age, but its expression was serene. Unlike the others, this statue didn't look like a noble figure or a wise elder. It was simple, unadorned, its eyes closed as if in contemplation.

Kai walked over to stand before it. Its base was surrounded by plain white flowers, unremarkable compared to the rest of the garden. She crouched beside it, examining the inscription carved into the stone:

The true path is the one that asks for nothing.

"I think this is the correct path," she said, standing. She looked at Liu. "The other paths are trying to distract us with what we think we want, but the one we need to follow is the one that doesn't offer us anything at all."

Liu regarded the path in silence. "This one doesn't have a glow, music, or anything. If what you say is true, then you're probably right."

Kai smiled, and without waiting for his response, she stepped onto the path lined with white flowers. The moment her foot touched the trail, the distant music stopped, and the shimmering allure of the other paths seemed to dim, as though the garden itself were retreating. Liu followed, his hand on the hilt of his sword, though there was no sense of immediate danger. The path twisted and turned, but the farther they walked, the quieter it became—no illusions, no temptations.

After what felt like ages, the white flowers thinned, and the path opened into a small clearing. At the center of the clearing stood an archway similar to the one they'd passed through before, but this one was overgrown with vines.

As they approached the archway, a soft voice whispered through the garden, barely audible but familiar. It was the same voice that had sung her mother's song earlier, but this time, it held no power over her. She glanced back at the winding paths they had left behind, the colors and lights fading into the twilight as they moved closer to the exit.

Kai stopped before the archway, her mind clearer now. She understood the garden's purpose—it had shown her that wisdom wasn't always about choosing the most obvious path or the one that promised the most reward. Sometimes, the best path was the one that offered nothing in return. It was a simple lesson, but it was a heavy truth.

The vines parted to reveal a dark passageway. Kai motioned to it and looked at Liu, smiling.

"I'll let you lead this time if you want."

Liu took a long look at her before responding. "Kokoro was right to send you here. You have a connection to the magic of this place. I will follow *your* lead."

Kai laughed and gazed ahead into the darkness. She couldn't shake the feeling that something dangerous lurked within, but she had successfully navigated through all the previous challenges. Surely this one couldn't be any worse than what they had faced so far... could it?

She stepped through the archway, and Liu followed her.

CHAPTER FOURTEEN

As Kai's eyes adjusted to the gloom, she saw they were in a circular chamber. The air hummed with an otherworldly energy that made the hairs on her arms stand on end. Before she could fully take in her surroundings, ethereal figures like the one from the first chamber materialized.

"We're surrounded," she whispered, grabbing the hilt of her sword. She doubted the weapon would do any good against the spirits, but the feel of it gave her a small measure of comfort.

The guardians raised their ghostly weapons in unison, their hollow voices echoing through the chamber.

"Prove your worth or perish."

The ground heaved, and from the earth rose several towering figures—golems, their bodies covered in the same ancient runes as the guardians. Kai unsheathed her sword and stepped backward.

"There's six of them," Liu said in disbelief.

Kai gripped her sword tighter, her eyes narrowing at the three golems that lumbered toward her. The other three went for Liu. The creatures gleamed with an unnatural green hue, and Kai suspected they were formed from jade. Their movements were slow but deliberate, and their weight caused the ground to shudder.

She considered how she might defeat them. Stone could be cracked, chipped, or broken, but jade—especially jade fused with magic—was a different challenge altogether.

Hikari's presence entered her mind. *They are not flesh and blood, but they have weaknesses. Find them, and you will bring them down.*

Kai wondered how the dragon knew what she faced, but she didn't have time to ask. The nearest golem raised its arm, the sound of creaking stone filling the air. It swung downward with terrifying speed, and Kai dove to the side just in time. The impact shook the ground, sending up a spray of dirt and shattered stone.

Liu was already on the move, his sword flashing in the dim light as he aimed for the joints of the golem closest to him. His blade met the jade with a metallic clang, but it barely left a scratch. He dodged a swing and back peddled.

"We need a strategy," he said.

Kai was back on her feet, her eyes flicking between the golems and the spectral guardians that now ringed the chamber. The runes etched onto the golems' jade surface emanated a soft shimmer, almost making the stone appear translucent.

"They are connected somehow," Kai said. "The golems and the spirits."

"What happens if you break that connection?"

Kai didn't know, but his question gave her an idea. One of the golems took a step toward her. She sprinted forward to meet it, slashing her sword at the glowing runes etched along its arm. Her sword sparked against the jade, and she felt the magic briefly flicker. That was it—the magic.

"Aim for the symbols," she shouted. "That's the key!"

Liu nodded, his face grim with focus. He darted past one golem, ducking beneath its heavy arm, and brought his blade down on the runes of its leg. The jade flared with a burst of light, and a deep crack appeared where his sword had struck.

"It's working," he said, dodging another swing. "We just need to—"

Before he could get the words out, another golem barreled forward, moving faster than its size suggested was possible. Its massive arm swung toward Liu, who barely had time to react. Kai's heart leaped into her throat as the blow connected, sending Liu flying backward. He crashed against the wall and slid to the ground, unconscious.

"Liu!"

Kai sprinted forward, her sword slicing through the air with precision. Her black blade connected with the largest rune on the first golem's chest, and a web of cracks spread across its torso. The golem faltered, its movements slowing as its magic began to unravel. That sent the others into a frenzy.

Ducking low, Kai ran to Liu's still form and stood in front of him. The golem Liu had struck drew closer, and Kai plunged her sword into the weak point he'd created in the creature's leg. With a loud crack, the limb shattered, sending the golem toppling to the ground with a deafening crash.

That left four still standing.

They wasted no time closing in. The guardians watched in silence, their gazes unwavering. Kai remained protectively in front of Liu's body, her mind racing for a plan to defeat the remaining golems.

Thinking about the cracks she had created in the first golem, Kai focused her attention on exploiting those weaknesses in the others. Ignoring the looming danger, she darted between the advancing golems, striking at their glowing runes. With each hit, cracks spiderwebbed across their jade bodies, the chamber echoing with every strike.

Kai fought with all the strength she could summon, but her energy was quickly fading. The weight of the situation pressed down on her, and she feared the end was near. Her breaths were labored and sweat made her clothes stick to her skin. She felt constricted, her movements growing sluggish.

She stumbled and fell, landing hard on the ground and her sword clattered as it bounced out of reach. Kai frantically searched for the magic that she had tapped into before, but it eluded her. The remaining golems advanced, and Kai saw her life flash before her eyes. She wanted to get up, to keep fighting, but her muscles felt like lead.

The massive creatures towered over her, and one of them raised its foot to crush her. Kai braced herself for the blow, but a battle cry startled her. She saw Liu on his feet, blood running down the side of his face from a wound on his head. He slammed his sword against the side of the golem about to step on Kai, which threw the creature off balance. It fell to the ground, and the others turned their attention to him.

Kai forced herself up and crawled on all fours to get to her sword. She snatched the blade up and stood, turning just in time to see the golems converge on Liu.

"No!"

He crumpled under their blows and lay still. Kai's vision blurred, and her arms trembled. She reached inward, feeling for the threads of magic that bound her to Hikari. At first, they slipped through her grasp. It was like trying to catch water in her hands. With a guttural shout, she tried again, and this time she managed to grab hold of it.

A surge of raw power erupted from her. It slammed into the golems, pinning them against the wall. Their runes flared as if trying to resist her, but they burned away under her fury, the magic roaring like an untamed fire. The agony of watching Liu fall had unlocked something primal within her.

The wave of energy caused the spectral guardians to flicker like candle flames caught in a breeze. With a sharp cry, Kai directed everything at the golems. Their jade bodies splintered into a thousand pieces, creating a deadly storm of shards as the debris whipped about the chamber.

Kai released the magic and staggered over to Liu's body. She dropped to her knees beside him, her hands trembling as she checked for a pulse. It was faint and quickly fading. Dread washed over her. He was dying, and it was all her fault.

CHAPTER FIFTEEN

"You have proven yourself worthy."

The guardian's words meant nothing. Tears blinded her, and she cursed herself for allowing Liu to come with her. If he'd have stayed behind with Kokoro...

You would be dead, Hikari said, her voice penetrating Kai's grief. *He sacrificed himself to save you.*

Kai wiped her tears away and looked at the guardian. It stood there impassively.

"Can you help him?" she asked.

"He is beyond all help."

Kai gasped and threw herself on top of Liu's body, tears falling freely. He had been more than a mentor to her, he had been her friend. Perhaps her only friend. Hikari's presence filled the bond, and a wave of comfort washed over her. It dulled the pain, but it didn't diminish it.

Time ceased to exist as she laid there. After a while, the tears stopped. She lifted her head to look for the guardians. They were gone, and in the center of the room stood a pedestal. Unfamiliar magic radiated from it, and Kai slowly stood. A shimmering mass of darkness sat atop the pedestal.

Kai approached cautiously, fearing there might be another test. She couldn't handle anything else. The cloak rippled like liquid night, its edges blurring and reforming in a mesmerizing pattern. Flecks of starlight danced across its surface, hinting at the vast power within its folds.

A conflicting mix of emotions churned within her. Kokoro said this cloak could help her defeat the Drakka, but at what cost? What would wielding such power do to her?

Power always comes with a price, Hikari told her. *But you have a pure heart and a just cause. If anyone can master it without being consumed, it's you.*

She sounded like Liu... the tears stung her eyes again, and she gritted her teeth against the pain. Pushing the agony aside, she grabbed the cloak. As soon as her fingers touched it, her eyes widened. The cloak seemed to be alive beneath her touch, its inky fabric undulating.

It's terrifying, she said.

Take it.

Kai lifted it from the pedestal. The weight of it surprised her. It felt both impossibly light and immeasurably heavy at the same time. With a fluid motion, she swung the cloak around her shoulders and drew it close. The moment it settled upon her, the world began to shift and blur. Darkness swirled at the edges of her vision, and she felt a peculiar sensation of being both present and elsewhere simultaneously.

Where did you go? Hikari's voice sounded distant, as if from underwater.

Kai struggled to focus, her perception constantly shifting between the physical world and something... other. Shadows danced around her, whispering secrets of ancient power and forgotten realms. She could sense the very fabric of reality bending and warping around her.

Hikari, can you hear me? It's overwhelming. I can see everything. The shadows, they're alive. And I can move through them, become one with them.

As she spoke, she felt herself slipping between realms, her body fading in and out of visibility. The boundaries where light and dark, physical and ethereal, blurred into meaninglessness. She was everywhere and nowhere, a being of shadow and substance.

This power is more than I could have imagined.

Control it, Hikari said, fear and awe mingling through the bond with her words. *You must control it.*

With a monumental effort of will, Kai forced herself to solidify, anchoring herself firmly in the physical realm. She squared her shoulders, and the cloak rippled around her like living darkness. She looked at Liu's body. The pain was still inside her, but it was distant now, as if many years had passed since his death.

"You deserve a better resting place than this," she said softly.

Kai lifted his body, cradling him in her arms. She thought he would be heavier, but perhaps she had grown stronger than she realized. Using the power of the cloak, she slipped into the shadow realm and walked through the walls, leaving the temple. She solidified and blinked against the harsh sunlight. Hikari regarded her curiously for a moment.

We will bury him at Tatenagawa, Kai said.

The dragon lowered her body so Kai could climb onto her back, and while still holding Liu's body, Kai heaved herself up, every muscle trembling. She situated herself and Hikari launched into the sky. The wind buffeted them, but Kai kept one hand tightly wrapped around Liu and the other held onto Hikari's scales.

How did you know what I faced in there? Kai asked.

We are bound as one. There were moments I could see through your eyes and hear what you heard.

Did you help me with any of the trials?

No, Hikari said solemnly. *I wanted to, but they forbade me.*

Who?

The guardians.

Kai sat in silence, her eyes tracing the shapes of Hikari's scales as she got lost in her thoughts. Liu had died to save her, and she would never forget that. With the Heart, and now the cloak, she would do whatever was necessary to bring an end to the Drakka.

The next two days seemed to last an eternity, but eventually, Tatenagawa grew visible in the distance, the temple rising like a dark sentinel against the horizon. Kai was relieved to see it, but she noticed smoke lazily curling into the air from one of the smaller courtyards.

Hikari roared and flapped her wings harder. Even from this distance, Kai knew the Drakka had returned. She prayed to her ancestors that Kokoro was safe, but something deep down told her the elder was in trouble.

As Hikari descended, Kai could see shattered statues and splintered gates. The temple grounds swarmed with Drakka, and there was no sign of Kokoro.

Do you sense her?

She is alive, but they have taken her captive. She says your sister is here.

CHAPTER SIXTEEN

Kai's heart skipped a beat. Akuhara was here? Rage and disbelief warred within her as Hikari began her descent.

Land away from the temple, Kai said.

Hikari obliged, taking them down near the river. They landed with a thud, and Kai slid off Hikari's back, her knees buckling for a moment beneath the weight of Liu's body. He seemed heavier now, and his limbs had stiffened at odd angles. She gently laid him on the grass, brushing a stand of hair from his face.

Stay here. I will find Kokoro and return.

Hikari rumbled her displeasure. *I will come with you.*

No. I can use the cloak to get in unseen, but the Drakka will spot you easily. I will be back as quickly as I can.

They stared at one another for a moment before Hikari nuzzled Kai in the chest.

If anything happens to you, I will destroy everything in my path.

Tears came unbidden to Kai's eyes at the dragon's words. She had never felt a love as deep as she shared with the dragon. Blinking the tears away, she rubbed the scales on Hikari's snout and turned toward the temple.

Smoke clung to the structure's eaves, curling into the sky like a serpent. The once-sacred grounds were now defiled with the presence of the Drakka. Kai balled her hands into fists, the cloak shifting around her, responding to the rise of her anger. The temple was almost unrecognizable, looking more like a battlefield than a place of peace.

Pulling the cloak tighter around her, Kai faded from view, slipping into the shadows. Her body became one with the darkness, the sensation disorienting her briefly. The cloak seemed to guide her, and she moved through the ruins like a wraith, her form shifting between realms.

She found Kokoro in the heart of the temple. Her wrists were bound together with a heavy, shimmering cord that pulsed with dark energy. Her face was pale, her eyes half-lidded.

"Kokoro," Kai whispered, materializing beside her.

The elder's eyes fluttered open, recognition flashing across her face. "You found it."

"I did. What happened here?"

"I tried to fight them off, but they're too strong. Your sister…"

"Where is she?"

Before Kokoro could respond, a slow, deliberate clap echoed through the chamber. Kai whirled around, her heart pounding.

There, standing at the far end of the room, was Akuhara.

"Little sister! Have you come to swear your loyalty to me?"

Kai drew her sword and scowled at the woman. They might share the same blood, but Akuhara was no sister to her. She wore the same dark robes as she had at Ikje. Behind her stood two hulking Drakka, their eyes full of malice.

"What are you doing here?"

"I'm cleaning the filth," Akuhara said, glancing behind her at Kokoro, her upper lip curling with disdain.

"I won't let you harm her."

Akuhara chuckled darkly, a sound that sent a shiver down Kai's spine. "What do you plan to do? If you stand in my way, you will die."

"Why are you helping them? They want nothing but destruction."

"You're a fool. Our mother spoiled you and made you weak. I don't help them, I *lead* them. And at my direction, they will change the order of things. The empire will crumble, and in its place will be something new, something better. You can be a part of it... if you bend the knee. Swear your allegiance to me."

"I will not bow to you," Kai said. "Ever."

"Then you have chosen death."

Akuhara drew her blade, a curved katana that gleamed as though it was forged from silver. The two women circled each other, the air between them as taut as a bowstring. They rushed forward at the same time, the clash of steel ringing out like a struck gong.

Kai gritted her teeth and slid her blade along Akuhara's in a shower of sparks, pushing back with a grunt of effort. Her sister smiled, twirling away and flicking her wrist. Dark tendrils of energy spiraled from her fingertips toward Kai's face. Without hesitation, Kai brought her blade up and blocked them. Her sword ignited with a brilliant orange light, devouring the tendrils.

Akuhara hissed and unleashed another spell. Kai leaped back just in time. The ground where she'd been exploded into a shower of black energy, jagged cracks spreading across the temple floor. Kai could feel something flowing through the bond, an ancient wisdom from elders long past. She extended her hand and flames erupted around her arm. Jerking her arm forward, the fire soared through the air in a blazing crescent.

Akuhara dodged to the side, summoning a magical shield that took the brunt of the damage. What remained of it continued onward, striking the wall next to one of the Drakka. The brute didn't budge other than to snarl. Kai closed the distance, her sword a blur of motion. She brought it down in an arc, aiming for Akuhara's exposed side.

The woman twisted her body at the last second, parrying the strike, then sent a blast of dark magic that sent Kai backward, her boots skidding across the cracked tiles. She winced, her muscles aching from the impact, but she regained her stance. Pulling from their bond, Kai channeled the power into a protective ring of fire around herself.

In a blur of motion, Akuhara darted forward, her dark magic snuffing out the flames as she crossed the barrier, jabbing her sword at Kai's stomach. Kai parried the strike, but Akuhara suddenly changed direction, her blade coming dangerously close to Kai's throat.

Kai leaned back so far she almost toppled over, but she managed to keep her balance and avoid being struck. She could feel her sword begging for the blood of the Drakka, and the cloak wanted her to submit herself to the shadow realm. It was almost too much.

Hikari's presence filled her mind, giving her renewed strength. She pushed the distracting whispers of her weapons aside and screamed. Flames enveloped her sword again. She attacked Akuhara relentlessly, pushing her back with every strike, her fiery blade leaving trails of scorched air in its wake.

Her sister snarled, frustration scrunching her face. With a wave of her hand, she summoned a dome of swirling black energy. It expanded outward, forcing Kai to back peddle as the dome writhed and twisted.

Kai narrowed her eyes, gripping her sword tighter. She took a deep breath, centering herself. Then, with a sharp exhale, she focused the flames to the tip of her sword. In one swift motion, she lunged forward, her sword cutting through the air like a comet. The flames roared, a concentrated beam of fire that pierced through Akuhara's dome, shattering it.

The force rippled through the air, sending the two Drakka slamming against the temple walls and blasting a hole to the outside. Stone and timber debris flew in every direction. Kai pressed on, slashing and jabbing Akuhara into a retreat that took them outside. Akuhara tripped and fell flat on her back. Kai stood over her and extinguished the flames from her sword, then pressed the tip of her blade against her sister's throat.

"It's over," Kai huffed.

Akuhara's lips curled into a smirk. "You've already lost and don't even know it."

A roar split the sky, and Kai snapped her head up to the heavens. A massive shape hurtled toward the courtyard. It was the gray dragon from Ikje, the one bonded to Akuhara. The dragon landed with a sound like a mountain breaking, and the shockwave sent Kai staggering.

I'm coming! Hikari shouted.

Drakka poured around the dragon's bulk, rushing to the aid of their leader. Akuhara rolled away, and wave of intense heat washed over Kai as the gray dragon unleashed his flames. Her first instinct was to fall into the shadow realm, but the Heart of Flame called to her, insistent. She acknowledged the stone, and as the flames reached her, they parted on either side, leaving her unscathed.

Akuhara's eyes widened briefly, and Kai found satisfaction in her surprise. She pulled the heart out of her bag and palmed it, then gripped the hilt of her sword. With the heart, the cloak, and the ancient magic that flowed through the bond, she felt as if nothing could stop her.

With a cry that didn't sound like her voice, Kai unleashed everything she could summon. Fire, earth, wind, water, shadow—they all converged. The sky darkened and the wind howled, bending trees. The earth split and heaved, and a maelstrom of fire erupted from the fissure, its tongues licking the sky. Lightning bolts blasted down from the sky, striking the gray dragon repeatedly. He roared in anger and pain. Akuhara staggered back, looking to her injured dragon.

Drakka fell into the fissure, burnt to ash within seconds. Kai wanted everything to burn, and she forced more power into the mix. The courtyard fell away into oblivion. This was the power of a true dragon rider, the power of the elements themselves. It was the power to destroy all that existed... but also to protect it.

Kai regained control of herself and stopped the magic. The winds began to die, and the flames subsided. The earth sealed back up, leaving a mark that resembled a scar.

"Retreat!" Akuhara screamed.

The Drakka that remained didn't need to be told twice. They fled, their withdrawal a disorganized, chaotic mess. Akuhara climbed onto her dragon's back and he leaped into the air. His scales were blackened in several spots, and he flapped his wings awkwardly.

Akuhara stared at her with hatred, and the dragon turned and left.

CHAPTER SEVENTEEN

Kai's body cried out for rest, but she went inside the temple and knelt beside Kokoro. The elder was alive, but barely. Her breathing was shallow, and she looked as though she were fading quickly. Hikari's bulk blotted out the light as she stuck her head through the ruins of the temple wall.

"Kokoro, you're safe now," Kai whispered, her voice hoarse and fragile. "They're gone."

"You're stronger than I thought you'd be."

"This power is more than I can handle."

"You will learn," Kokoro replied, each word a labor of effort. "Speak the oaths."

Kai's brow furrowed in confusion. "What?"

"The... oaths..."

Kai realized what she meant, and she glanced at Hikari. *Do you know the words?*

They are inscribed in my blood.

Kai nodded and turned back to Kokoro. She brushed soot-stained hair from the elder's face, her touch tender, almost fearful, as if she were afraid to hurt her. Kokoro's eyes slid shut, and for a moment, Kai thought she was gone. Kokoro spoke again, but it was barely above a whisper.

"Hurry…"

"By the sacred flame and the ancient bond we share, I vow to uphold the honor of our ancestors, to protect our lands and its people with courage and wisdom. With my dragon as my guide and my strength, I pledge my life to the guardianship of our realm, now and for all eternity."

By the breath of fire and the skies we soar, I vow to honor our ancient bond, to protect our lands and its creatures with might and grace. With my rider as my heart and my spirit, I pledge my life to the guardianship of our realm, now and for all eternity.

"You… are no… longer… Chosen. You… are… Sworn."

A final breath escaped Kokoro's lips, and she went still. Kai wanted to cry, but no tears would come. There would be a time for them, she knew, but it was not now. She stood, her movements slow. Exhaustion threatened to overtake her, but she pushed through it. There was one more thing to be done before she could rest. She needed to bury her friends.

Hikari dug two deep graves, and Kai placed Liu's body in one and Kokoro's in the other. She stared at them for a long moment, not knowing what to say. There were no witnesses other than Hikari, but it felt wrong to say nothing. Eventually, she decided on her words.

"You have found peace from this world. I will hold you in my heart, grateful for the time we shared. Thank you for everything you taught me."

She nodded at Hikari, and the dragon filled the graves with dirt, using her claws to pack it down tightly.

Where do we go from here?

Kai turned her gaze to the horizon, in the direction Akuhara had fled.

We go to end this, once and for all.

RICHARD FIERCE

SWORN

BOUND BY BLOOD BOOK 3

CHAPTER ONE

Akuhara stood atop a cliff overlooking the Drakka encampment, her dark armor glinting in the light of hundreds of campfires scattered across the valley below. The air was thick with the scent of smoke, and she wrinkled her nose at the smell. Her dragon lay coiled beside her as she gazed out at the horde with a mixture of pride and unease.

The encampment was a chaotic sprawl of tents, sharpened stakes, and roving Drakka. Their guttural growls and hissing filled the air, a discordant symphony that grated against Akuhara's thoughts. She could see them moving in restless clusters, sharpening weapons, devouring raw meat, and occasionally snapping at one another. They were powerful, yes, but undisciplined, unruly. Her magic was the only thing keeping them in line.

She inhaled deeply, the weight of this war pressing down on her.

What do you suppose they think of me? she wondered, her gaze lingering on a pair of Drakka snarling over a scrap of meat.

They fear you, her dragon rumbled, its voice a low growl that resonated in her mind like thunder. *As they should.*

Akuhara's lips twisted into a bitter smile. *Fear is a powerful tool. It keeps them obedient. But it's not enough.*

The dragon tilted its head, smoke curling from its nostrils. Its eyes narrowed as it studied her. *Doubt lingers in your heart. Why?*

Akuhara's hand clenched into a fist. Her nails bit into her palm, the pain grounding her. *Because this wasn't how it was supposed to be. I wanted to rebuild, to create something better. But these... creatures... they only understand destruction.*

Her words hung in the air, and the dragon's gaze didn't waver. *Destruction is the path to rebirth,* it said finally, its tone edged with impatience. *To create something better, you must first sweep away what is broken.*

Akuhara turned away, her jaw tight. Her gaze drifted to the horizon, where the flickering lights of a distant city dotted the landscape like fireflies in the night. The sight stirred something deep within her—a memory, unbidden and unwelcome.

The air in the gardens had always smelled of jasmine and freshly turned soil, a heady mix that still lingered in Akuhara's mind even now. She had been no more than eight, crouched behind a cluster of towering azaleas, her knees pressed into the damp earth as she peered through the gaps in the leaves. Ahead, a girl stood in the sunlight, a wooden training sword gripped tightly in her hands.

The girl—Kai—moved with unpolished determination, swinging the sword in wide arcs. Her brow furrowed in concentration, and sweat glistened on her forehead as her breath came in quick, sharp bursts. Beside her, an imposing man stood with his arms crossed, his expression stern yet proud as he corrected her stance.

"Again," he commanded, his deep voice carrying across the garden.

Kai nodded and adjusted her grip, her small frame trembling with effort. She was so focused, so utterly absorbed in the task, that she didn't notice Akuhara watching. No one did.

Akuhara remained hidden, pressing herself further into the shadows of the azaleas. She wasn't supposed to be there. She wasn't supposed to exist. Left behind at birth, presumed dead, she had been swept away into the embrace of the Drakka. And yet, drawn by curiosity or some unnameable force, she had found her way back here, to this garden, to this girl who shared her face.

As Kai completed another swing, the man stepped forward, placing a hand on her shoulder. "Good. But strength alone isn't enough. You must learn to anticipate, to see what comes next."

Kai looked up at him, her eyes wide with determination. "I will. I'll make you proud."

Akuhara's chest tightened. Pride. Approval. These were things she had never known, raised as she was among creatures who valued only destruction. Watching this moment felt like gazing into a life that could have been hers, a life stolen from her the moment she was cast aside.

Her nails dug into the damp earth. She wanted to step out from her hiding place, to confront the man, the girl. To demand answers. But what would she say? That she was the daughter they abandoned? The child they never knew?

She turned away, her small hands curling into fists. Even at that age, the bitterness had already begun to take root, twisting through her like the tendrils of dark magic she would one day wield. But alongside it was something else, something softer. A yearning to be seen, to be acknowledged, even if only from the shadows.

"One day," she whispered to herself, the words barely audible. "One day, they'll know."

The memory faded as quickly as it had come, leaving Akuhara standing on the cliff once more, the scent of jasmine replaced by smoke and ash. She closed her eyes, exhaling a slow, measured breath.

Perhaps, she said, her tone softer now, tinged with a weariness she couldn't entirely suppress. *But sometimes, I can't help but wonder...*

Her dragon shifted beside her, its massive form blocking out the campfires below. *Your sister is a weakness,* it hissed, the venom in its tone unmistakable. *She clings to a broken world. You are stronger without her.*

Akuhara didn't respond immediately. Instead, she knelt and placed her hand on the earth. The ground beneath her palm was cold, unyielding. Tendrils of dark energy seeped from her fingertips, snaking into the soil like roots of a malignant tree. The Drakka nearest to her stiffened, their eyes sharpening into focus as her magic strengthened their bond. She felt their fear, their hunger, their rage—all of it feeding into her power, bolstering her control.

They follow because they fear, Akuhara said, her eyes fixed on the writhing energy beneath her hand. *But fear can turn to defiance. We must act soon before the tide shifts.*

The dragon loomed closer, its massive head lowering to her level. Wisps of smoke drifted from its nostrils, and its eyes burned like embers. *Then give the order,* it rumbled. *Let the cities burn. Let their hope turn to ash.*

Akuhara stood, her expression hardening. She raised her hand, the dark energy crackling around her. *No more waiting,* she said. *We march at dawn.*

CHAPTER TWO

The sky burned crimson, streaked with black smoke that blotted out the stars. Kai stood in the center of the battlefield, her hands trembling as she gripped her sword. Around her, the ground was littered with the fallen, their faces obscured by ash. The stench of blood and charred flesh choked the air, but it was the silence that pressed down on her like a vice. Not a single cry or groan of pain, only the crackle of distant flames and the low rumble of something vast moving in the shadows.

"Hikari?" Kai called, her voice hoarse and small against the oppressive stillness. She turned, searching for the gleam of her dragon's gold scales.

A shadow shifted, and she froze. Emerging from the smoke was Akuhara, her twin sister, clad in dark armor that shimmered with magic like oil on water. Her dragon loomed behind her, its eyes glowing a sickly green, its scales blackened and twisted as if burned from the inside.

Akuhara smiled, a cruel twist of her lips. "Did you really think you could stop me, sister?"

Kai raised her sword, but her hands shook. "I won't let you destroy everything."

"Oh, Kai," Akuhara said, her voice dripping with mockery. "You already have." She gestured around them, and Kai's heart dropped as she saw the faces of the dead. Ryn, Master Satoshi, the Sundered—all staring at her with lifeless eyes, blame etched into their features.

"No," Kai whispered, taking a step back. "This isn't real."

Akuhara laughed, a chilling sound that echoed across the battlefield.

The ground trembled as Hikari emerged from the smoke, but something was wrong. Her scales were streaked with veins of black, her eyes clouded with the same sickly green light as Akuhara's dragon.

"Hikari?" Kai's voice cracked. She reached out a hand, but the dragon snarled, baring fangs that dripped with venom.

"She's mine now," Akuhara said, stepping closer. "You were never strong enough to be her rider."

Hikari reared back, her massive wings casting Kai in shadow. Then, with a deafening roar, the dragon lunged.

Kai screamed as darkness swallowed her.

She jolted awake, her breath coming in ragged gasps. Her hands clawed at the dragon skin cloak she had wrapped around herself, the Heart of Flame pulsing faintly at her side. For a moment, she didn't recognize her surroundings— a campfire's dim glow, the quiet rustle of trees. Hikari lay a short distance away, her scales gleaming softly in the moonlight as she slept.

Kai pressed a trembling hand to her chest, willing her racing heart to calm. It was just a dream. A nightmare. But the fear lingered, curling in her gut like a living thing.

Hikari stirred, her eyes opening to meet Kai's. *What's wrong?* the dragon asked, her voice a low rumble in Kai's mind.

Kai shook her head, unable to find her voice. She glanced at the sword lying beside her, echoes of the nightmare flashing in her mind.

It's nothing, she said finally, though the words felt hollow. *Just... a dream.*

Hikari tilted her head, her gaze piercing. *Dreams often reveal truths we try to ignore.*

Kai swallowed hard, the image of Hikari's twisted form still vivid in her mind. She looked away, staring into the dying embers of the fire.

We should get moving, she said, her thoughts steadier now. *Akuhara's out there, and I... I won't let that dream become reality.*

Hikari huffed softly, a plume of smoke curling from her nostrils. *Then let us ensure it does not.*

Kai nodded. The nightmare had shaken her, but it had also ignited something deeper—a determination to face her sister, no matter the cost.

She crawled over to the fire, brushing her fingers through the dirt to extinguish the last of the embers. The faint crackle died away, leaving only the chirp of crickets and the occasional rustle of leaves in the night. She stood, slinging the dragon skin cloak over her shoulders, its weight and warmth a reassuring presence against the chill of the night air.

Hikari rose to her feet, stretching her wings wide. The moonlight caught on her scales, and for a moment, Kai found solace in the sight.

We continue East, Kai said. *To Ikje.*

Hikari lowered herself, allowing Kai to climb onto her back. The familiar feel of the dragon's scales beneath her hands comforted her, pushing away the tendrils of the nightmare that tried to claw at her mind. With a mighty beat of her wings, Hikari launched into the air, the ground falling away beneath them. The wind rushed past Kai's face, cold and carrying the scent of pine.

As they soared higher, the stars came into view. Their distant glow would soon vanish, as dawn was nearing.

Kai tightened her grip on Hikari's neck, her gaze fixed on the horizon. They flew for a while in silence until Kai spotted a small village, its wooden houses clustered together. No smoke rose from chimneys, and the silence was unnatural, thick and stifling.

Something feels wrong, Kai said, her right hand instinctively going to the hilt of her sword. She patted Hikari's neck. *Take us down.*

The dragon rumbled in agreement and descended. Her claws kicked up dust as she landed at the edge of the village. Kai slid from Hikari's back, her boots crunching against the dirt. The air was still—too still. Even the usual chirping of crickets was absent.

Kai scanned the empty streets, then cautiously stepped toward the nearest house, its door hanging ajar. Inside, overturned furniture and shattered pottery told a story of sudden violence.

The faint scent of blood reached her nose, metallic and sharp. Her stomach turned, but she pressed forward, her blade drawn. Outside, Hikari's low growl drew Kai's attention to the shadows beyond the village square. Movement. A flicker of light reflected off dark, scaled bodies.

"Drakka!" she shouted as the creatures burst from their hiding places.

The first Drakka lunged, its claws slashing through the air. Kai sidestepped and swung her blade in a clean arc, slicing through its neck. The creature's lifeless body crumpled to the ground, but more took its place, their guttural snarls filling the silence.

The Drakka moved with eerie coordination, flanking Kai as they pressed her toward the square. She parried one strike, her sword clanging against the creature's talons, then ducked another swipe aimed at her head. A third Drakka lunged from her left, and she barely twisted out of its reach.

Hikari roared, unleashing a torrent of flame that lit up the square. The fire scattered the Drakka, some of them shrieking as their scales blackened and cracked. They regrouped quickly, swarming from alleys and rooftops. Kai's mind raced. There were too many of them.

Hikari, the ridge! she called, pointing to a narrow ledge above the village. If she could collapse it, it would crush the Drakka below.

Hikari launched into the air, her wings beating powerfully. Kai darted between attackers, slashing and parrying as she made her way to higher ground. The Drakka pursued, their talons gouging the earth as they climbed after her. She reached a crumbling staircase carved into the cliffside, her legs burning as she sprinted upward. Below, the Drakka surged forward, their eyes fixed on her.

From above, Hikari dropped a boulder onto the ridge. The rock groaned and splintered, cracks spiderwebbing across its surface. Kai pressed herself against the cliff wall as a thunderous crash echoed through the valley. Tons of rock tumbled down, crushing the Drakka in a cloud of dust and debris.

Breathing heavily, Kai looked down at the devastation. The ground was littered with broken bodies and shattered stones. Hikari landed beside her.

We need to keep moving, Kai said, wiping blood from her sword. *There could be more.*

As they took to the skies, Kai cast one last glance at the ruined village. She spotted movement among the rubble— one Drakka, barely alive, dragging itself from beneath the rocks. Its eyes met hers for a brief moment before Hikari's shadow enveloped it, and Kai turned away.

They flew in silence, the ambush weighing on her. *They're getting more intentional,* Kai finally said. *That didn't feel random.*

No, Hikari agreed. *Someone is watching us.*

Kai's thoughts darkened. Akuhara. Her sister's shadow loomed over every move the Drakka made, every life they destroyed. She clenched her jaw.

She will pay for all of her crimes.

CHAPTER THREE

Ikje had fallen.

Kai's stomach lurched as Hikari circled over the scorched ruin. The once-impenetrable city had been reduced to rubble, its stone walls toppled and its streets abandoned. Charred remains of houses stood like skeletal sentinels, their wooden beams cracked and blackened. The place resembled that of a graveyard more than a city.

We're too late, Kai said, feeling her throat constrict.

A part of her had hoped, naively perhaps, that Ikje would somehow survive the onslaught. As she took in the collapsed towers and the vast emptiness where markets had been, she realized that hope was a fragile thing.

Take us lower, she bade Hikari.

The dragon banked sharply, her wings cutting through the air as they descended toward the city. As they approached, the stench of ash and death grew stronger. Kai swallowed hard. She had never seen such destruction, but it was more than that. This... this was personal. Her parents had been here. Had they managed to escape, or had she lost them as she had lost Liu and Kokoro?

Hikari landed softly amid the wreckage of what had been the main square where the Ceremony of Oaths had taken place. Kai slid from the dragon's back and landed on the cobblestones with a thud, her boots stirring up clouds of soot. Her eyes flicked over the debris. All around her, the silence was oppressive. There were no signs of survivors, but Kai decided to search anyway.

"Hello? Is anyone here?"

She wandered among the ruins and stopped near a half-destroyed fountain. The water was long gone, replaced by dust and ash. In its center, the stone figure of a dragon still stood, though its face was cracked and broken.

Kai continued to pick her way through the ruins. She may not have been able to prevent this tragedy, but she would do everything in her power to ensure it never happened again. Her cloak flapped in the wind as she walked, darker than the blackened stones beneath her feet.

A sudden movement caught her eye. Her head snapped up, and she caught a glimpse of a figure walking among the rubble. Without hesitation, she sprinted ahead, Hikari following close behind.

"Wait!" Kai called.

The figure turned, and Kai's breath caught in her throat. It was an elderly woman, her face streaked with soot. She clutched a rag to her face, and her eyes widened with terror at the sight of Hikari.

Kai lifted her hands in a gesture of peace. "We're not here to hurt you."

The woman hesitated, her gaze darting between Kai and Hikari. "The Drakka," she rasped. "They did this."

"I know. Is there anyone else here?"

The woman shook her head. "Those who survived went to Dangju."

Kai remembered Master Satoshi commanding the Sworn to flee there during the attack, but it didn't make sense for everyone to go there. Zhencheng was closer.

"We can take you to Dangju. Do you have family there?"

"My family is gone," the woman replied. "They died here fighting the Drakka."

"I'm sorry." Kai felt helpless, and she looked at Hikari. "We can take you somewhere else, somewhere safe."

"This place is safe. The Drakka have already destroyed it. I doubt they will come back. Leave me be, child, and do what you must."

"Can you tell me where Dangju is?"

"Go east. It's on the coast."

The woman walked away, and Kai sighed. She could force the woman to come with them, but she didn't feel that was the right thing to do. She watched the woman until she disappeared behind the remnants of a building, then she turned to Hikari.

We need to stop Akuhara before she destroys another city, but we can't do it alone. We need the other Sworn.

The dragon rumbled her agreement. *We can leave now, but what of the Sundered? They'll be here soon.*

We'll backtrack and let them know to continue on to Dangju. It'll take them longer than us to get there, but they can catch up.

Hikari lowered herself to the ground and Kai climbed up her shoulder. With a powerful thrust of her wings, the dragon launched into the air. The ruins of Ikje spread out beneath them like a grim tapestry of destruction. Kai leaned forward, her fingers gripping Hikari's scales as they soared west. They didn't have to fly far before the Sundered came into view.

There, Kai said, pointing. *They're making good time.*

Hikari descended, landing far ahead of them so she didn't scare their horses. Kai remained on the dragon's back, waiting for the Sundered to draw nearer. Ryn was leading the group, and he dismounted, handing the reins to one of the others.

"What's wrong?" he asked as he approached.

"Ikje is gone," Kai answered. "We're going to Dangju instead."

"Gone? How? Its walls have never been breached before."

"I know. With Akuhara leading them, the Drakka have become an organized force. It seems nothing can stop them." Kai paused, unsure how Ryn would react to her next words. "Master Satoshi and some of the other Sworn are in Dangju. I know you don't care for the empire, but we're stronger together."

Ryn stared at her in silence. Finally, he nodded. "I can't guarantee the others will come, but I swore an oath of loyalty to you. I will go where you go."

"You willingly gave that oath. I did not request it, nor will I require you to fulfill it. But I would be grateful if you fight alongside the Sworn with me. The same goes for the others." She nodded toward the Sundered who waited behind him.

"We fight as one for the sake of our fallen dragons," Ryn said. "We will meet you in Dangju."

"Thank you. I will see you in a few days, then. May your travels be safe."

Ryn bowed his head and returned to his horse. Hikari took to the air again, flying east this time. The wind whipped through Kai's hair, and for a moment, she forgot about the world below and reveled in the feeling of flight.

Hours passed, marked only by the gradual movement of the sun across the sky. Kai's muscles ached from the prolonged flight, but she refused to complain. Instead, she focused on the changing landscape below, using it to distract herself from the fatigue.

I've never seen this part of the empire before, she told Hikari.

Do you see that formation of rocks?

Kai peered down, spotting an unusual circular arrangement of boulders. *What is it?*

An old nesting ground. Long abandoned, but once home to my kind.

Dragons in general, or elders?

Elders.

Kai stared at the place in awe, but a hint of sadness overtook her for the loss of the elders. Hikari was the last one. What did that mean? Would something happen to the world at Hikari's passing? She was hopeful that day wouldn't come for many years, but the thoughts plagued her regardless.

Over the course of the next two days, the landscape gradually transformed. Tall mountains and lush forests gave way to rocky cliffs, and the distant shimmer of the coast appeared on the horizon. A gust of wind slammed into them, nearly unseating Kai. She pressed herself close to Hikari's neck and held on tighter.

The coastal winds are strong, but we survived a storm. This is nothing!

Hikari roared and beat her wings harder, fighting against the turbulent air. The gusts came sporadically, making a steady flight impossible. They pressed onward, leaving the cliffs behind and finding sprawling hills that eventually flattened to grassy plains. In the distance, Kai could see smoke, but it was too faint to be from an attack.

I think that's Dangju, Kai said.

The city came into view, and the first thing Kai noticed was the city's defenses were more robust than Ikje's. The walls stood high, lined with ballistae, and from her vantage point, she could make out rows of soldiers moving about in formations.

Beyond the city, the blue waters of the Bay of Five Winds lapped against the shore. Boats were docked at the nearby harbor, and the smoke she had seen earlier rose from chimneys scattered throughout the city. The air was thick with the scent of salt and fish, and she felt Hikari's stomach rumble with hunger.

A horn blared, and Kai scanned the city walls to see several ballistae turn and take aim at them. Kai straightened and waved one arm in the air.

Hold on, Hikari said.

Kai's eyes widened as the soldiers launched several bolts. They whizzed past them, barely missing their mark.

Land, quickly! she urged.

Hikari dipped her wings and dove toward the ground. Kai hoped their arrival wouldn't face any further hostility if they landed outside of the city. They touched down near the gates, and a host of Sworn flew over the walls, surrounding them.

"Stay your weapons," a familiar voice shouted. "It's Kai Lin."

CHAPTER FOUR

The cavernous nest deep beneath the earth pulsed with life. The walls of the chamber shimmered faintly, streaked with glowing veins of molten energy, and the air was thick with the heat and dampness of the underground. At the edges of the room, clusters of Drakka eggs lay nestled in shallow pits, their translucent shells glowing faintly with the promise of life. The sound of their faint, rhythmic pulsations mingled with the guttural growls of the generals who surrounded Akuhara.

She stood at the center of the chamber, a crude stone table before her. Her dragon stood behind her, its molten eyes glowing in the dimness. Akuhara raised her hands, summoning a swirl of dark energy that coalesced into a flickering map of the empire. Mountain ranges and rivers glimmered faintly, marked by the strategic locations she had chosen. The Drakka generals leaned forward, their eyes fixed on the projection.

"Xeroth, Kalrek," Akuhara growled in their guttural tongue, her voice filled with authority. The two largest

Drakka stepped forward, their hulking forms towering over her. "Your forces will divide."

She pointed to the glowing map, tracing a path toward Dangju. "Xeroth, you will take half of the army southeast. Burn Dangju to the ground. Leave no survivors." The Drakka rumbled in approval. "Once the city demolished, you will meet us here."

Her hand shifted to Zhencheng, the imperial capital, where the lights of the empire still burned defiantly. "Kalrek, the other half marches with you and me to Zhencheng. We will crush their heart and extinguish their hope."

The generals snarled in excitement, their guttural cries reverberating through the cavern. Akuhara's dragon mirrored their satisfaction. She projected confidence, but beneath her commanding exterior, unease gnawed at Akuhara's resolve.

The resistance they had faced was stronger than she had anticipated. She couldn't shake the feeling that these attacks would only serve to unite the empire, not break it apart. Splitting her forces was risky, but she would shield the Drakka that traveled to the imperial city with her magic, hiding them from prying eyes until it was too late for the emperor to stop them.

As the generals left to ready their forces, Akuhara lingered in the cavern. She stared at the flickering map, her fingers brushing against the glowing outline of Zhencheng. She knew she was walking a dangerous path, but with each passing day, her grip on power tightened, and the whispers of fear that followed her name grew louder.

But there was one person whose voice still rang clear in her mind: her sister. She couldn't forget the look of triumph in Kai's eyes during their last battle. Akuhara couldn't help but feel a sense of dread at the thought of facing her again.

Her dragon spoke, shattering her thoughts. *The Drakka hunger for blood. You cannot control them forever.*

"I know," Akuhara whispered aloud. She closed her eyes, exhaling slowly. *Once the empire is ash, their purpose will end. And so will they.*

The dragon's eyes glowed brighter, its voice laced with curiosity. *You would destroy them? Your own kin?*

Akuhara turned to face the beast, her expression hard. *They are not my kin. They are a means to an end.*

The dragon hissed but said nothing more. Akuhara turned back to the map. She had no illusions about the Drakka's nature. They were creatures of chaos, incapable of building the world she envisioned. But the thought of what must come after filled her with dread.

Her voice was a whisper as she stared at the flickering map. "The empire deserves to fall, but I will not trade one tyranny for another. When the time comes, I will find a way to end the Drakka."

The dragon growled softly behind her, its presence a constant reminder of the storm she had unleashed. Akuhara's gaze remained fixed on the map, her resolve hardening like steel. There was no turning back now. To rebuild, she would have to destroy everything—including the monsters that had taken her in.

CHAPTER FIVE

Relief washed over Kai as she stared at Siran. It had only been a few weeks since they had parted ways, but the woman looked as different as Kai felt inwardly. She glanced at the other Sworn and saw Jiro, Ichiro, Kazu, and the others from Ikje. She nodded to each of them and turned back to Siran.

"The guards seem on edge," she said.

"They are. A Drakka army is heading this way as we speak. Our scouts are tracking their movements."

"I didn't see anything on the way here. Which direction are they coming from?"

"The north. They'll be here by nightfall." Siran looked from Kai to Hikari. "This isn't the dragon from the ceremony."

"No, she isn't. This is Hikari."

Siran bowed her head to the dragon. "Master Satoshi will want to see you. He sent a message to Tatenagawa but never received a reply. We feared the worst."

"I'm fine, but..." Kai clenched her jaw. "Things will only get worse if we don't stop the Drakka once and for all."

"Come," Siran said. "I will take you to Master Satoshi."

Siran and the other Sworn took to the air and flew over the wall. Hikari followed them, and Kai looked down at the city. It was a sprawling metropolis, with shops and markets bustling with people. Soldiers manned the watchtowers, keeping a vigilant watch over the landscape. If she didn't know any better, Kai would have no idea the city was preparing for an assault.

They landed outside a massive complex that served as the barracks. Kai swung a leg over Hikari's side and dropped to the ground.

"Your dragon can find food and water here," Siran said. "She can also rest in any of the open stables."

I'll be back soon, Kai told Hikari, running a hand along the dragon's neck. Hikari nuzzled her in return, and Kai fell into step beside Siran. The streets were crowded with both soldiers and civilians, but Siran parted the throng with authority.

"Are you in charge of the Sworn?" Kai asked.

Siran looked at her questioningly. Her expression shifted from confusion to a smile. "No, I am not. I would like to lead one day, assuming we survive."

Kai returned the smile, but she didn't like Siran's dark words. They had to survive. They were the empire's only defense.

"They've fortified the city well," Kai said. "But it will take more than walls to hold back the Drakka."

"We've been preparing while also training. It hasn't been easy, and most of the others still aren't ready, but we've run out of time. They are moving more quickly than we expected."

"That's because they have a leader now."

"What do you mean?"

"You know, don't you? The woman who took my dragon at the ceremony is behind all of this."

"Your twin sister?"

"Yes. She is aligned with the Drakka and leads them. That's why they are more organized now."

They approached a grand structure with towering columns and intricate carvings that blended the empire's martial heritage with artistic elegance. The heavy doors swung open as they neared, and Siran took the lead, guiding Kai through the hallways to a large chamber where a group of people were gathered around a circular table.

Master Satoshi looked up, meeting Kai's gaze. She bowed her head to him and said, "We need to talk."

He immediately dismissed his council, Siran included. Once the room was cleared, the two stood in silence for a long moment before Master Satoshi spoke.

"You are different. Your *ki* radiates strength, and I sense a powerful aura of magic. Tell me everything."

Kai obeyed, relaying everything that had happened to her since she'd originally left Ikje. Master Satoshi frowned briefly when she mentioned bonding with Hikari, but otherwise, he listened intently without speaking. When she pulled the Heart of Flame out of her silk bag, its pulsing light cast an otherworldly glow across the room. She held it up for him to see, and her cloak billowed of its own accord.

"The legends are true," Master Satoshi said, his expression grave. His eyes, usually sharp and discerning, now held a mix of awe and deep-seated worry.

"I did not think such artifacts were real. The power you wield is beyond anything I've encountered in all my years. Your bond... it is both a gift and a curse."

"What do you mean?"

"Power always comes at a price, Kai. And bonding with an elder dragon..." He trailed off, shaking his head. "It is forbidden for a reason. This gemstone and cloak, too, carry their own dangers. Together, they make you a formidable force, but also a target."

Kai's brow furrowed. "A target? For whom?"

"For those who fear power they cannot control," Master Satoshi replied grimly. "The emperor himself would view this as a threat to his authority."

The weight of his words crashed down upon her. Her chest tightened, and she swallowed hard before asking, "What would happen if the emperor found out?"

Master Satoshi lowered his voice despite there being no one else in the chamber. "It means certain death, not just for you and your dragon, but for any who know of your bond."

Deep down, Kai knew the answer before he confirmed it. She clenched her hands into fists to keep them from shaking. "But I am fighting *for* the empire. Eradicating the Drakka is my sole concern. I never meant to put anyone in danger. My bond with Hikari... it feels right, as if it was meant to be. How can something so powerful, so pure, be wrong?"

"The emperor won't see it that way. He will see you as a threat, and he will act accordingly. That is why he can never know."

"What?" Kai's eyes widened in surprise.

"We must keep it a secret, no matter the cost," Master Satoshi replied.

Kai took a deep breath and met his intense gaze. She couldn't believe he was vowing to deceive the emperor. He barely knew her, and yet he was willing to risk his position, and even his life, for her.

"Thank you, Master. If I can help prevent more bloodshed, then I'm willing to face whatever consequences may come. Please do not risk your life for me. If the emperor finds out, tell him you didn't know."

"Your courage is commendable. Have you told anyone else?"

"No. Liu was the only one, and..." Kai trailed off, and Master Satoshi took her hand in his.

"Liu was a great warrior. He died protecting you, as was his duty. His sacrifice will not be forgotten."

Kai knew his words were sincere, and she nodded. "Siran said there is an army of Drakka headed here. What can I do to help?"

"Fight, when the time comes. We have done everything we can to prepare. Now, we wait."

CHAPTER SIX

As night fell, the glow of torches illuminated the city. Kai stood at the top of one of the many watchtowers, her eyes turned upward to the vast expanse of stars overhead. The cool night air was a welcome reprieve from the heat, and she heaved a sigh.

"Do you think it will be enough?" she asked, looking at Siran. Kai had volunteered to keep watch with her, mainly because she couldn't sleep. Her nerves were too on edge, and the anticipation of what was to come kept her mind racing.

"It has to be," Siran replied. "If we fall—"

"We won't," Kai interrupted. "We can't. I just meant... I don't know. I hope we're ready."

"Readiness is a luxury rarely afforded in times of war, but we are as ready as we can be." They were silent for a moment before Siran continued. "Forgive me. I don't mean for my words to sound so dark. I have seen more death than I care to, and there will be more to come before it is all over. It weighs heavily on me."

"I understand."

Kai turned her gaze to the sky again, tracing the familiar constellations. The Hunter, The Dragon, The Imperial Crown. They glowed clearly in the heavens, constant and unchanging despite the chaos that brewed far below them.

The sound of thunder drew Kai's attention to the north. It hadn't looked like it would rain earlier, but she quickly realized it wasn't a storm approaching. A dark mass appeared on the horizon, growing larger with each passing moment.

Siran scrambled to her feet and alerted the city by ringing the enormous bell atop the tower. The noise echoed into the night, and the other watchtowers soon joined in the warning. Kai watched as the mass drew steadily closer, the endless ranks of Drakka causing the very ground to tremble.

They are here, Kai told Hikari. *I'm coming to you.*

She raced down the stairs of the tower, sprinting through the empty streets to the barracks. Hikari was already out of the stable, and she lowered herself to the ground so Kai could climb onto her back.

"Sworn, to your mounts!" Master Satoshi's voice rang out.

In a flurry of motion, riders took to the sky, circling above the city. Kai and Hikari joined them, watching as the first wave of Drakka crashed against the walls like a tidal wave. The creatures clawed their way up the stonework, but they were met with sword and spear as the soldiers on the parapets hacked and stabbed at them.

Kai could feel the tension in Hikari's body, a coiled spring waiting for the right moment to strike. Kai patted the dragon's neck.

Wait for the signal, she said.

The air filled with the sounds of battle. Clanging metal, screams, and the roars of Drakka intertwined into a cacophony of noise. Kai's heart pounded in her chest as she watched the conflict unfold. The soldiers fought bravely, but the sheer number of Drakka threatened to overwhelm them.

"Defend the walls!"

She barely heard Master Satoshi's command over the wind, and Hikari was flying toward the wall before Kai realized what was happening. She drew her blade and held on tightly as the dragon dove down sharply, pulling up at the last second to latch her rear claws onto the top of the battlements.

A flap of her wings sent a gust of wind into the nearest Drakka, and they went tumbling backward. Hikari opened her jaws and unleashed a torrent of flames. The fire lit up the night, and Kai's eyes widened. The Drakka's numbers were beyond counting. The acrid smell of burning flesh in her nostrils broke her reverie, and she glanced along the wall.

Archers loosed volleys of arrows, and the other soldiers fought with everything they had. She caught sight of a few faces. Their eyes were wide with fear, but they fought on, knowing the cost of failure. A Drakka scaled the wall, climbing over the top and attacking a young soldier.

Without thinking, Kai leaped from Hikari's back and slashed the creature across its back with her sword. The Drakka howled in pain and fury as it recoiled, giving the soldier time to regain his wits and launch his own attack. Together, they backed the creature against the wall, where Hikari promptly swatted it into the air. Its roar faded among the noise, and the soldier offered Kai a grateful nod before returning to the wall and slashing at more Drakka.

There is something out there, Hikari said.

What is it?

I'm not sure. It feels like a dragon, but it's… different.

Kai looked out at the sea of Drakka, but nothing stood out. Then she heard it. A deep, resonating roar that vibrated the air around her. In the distance, a shadowy form emerged. It towered over the Drakka, larger and more sinister than anything she'd seen before. Its eyes burned with malevolence, and Kai was overwhelmed with terror.

She stood frozen in place, unable to tear her gaze away from the dragon-like beast. Its scales were black as midnight and seemed to swallow the surrounding light. The soldiers around her faltered, their movements slowing as they caught sight of the colossal beast. Kai's fear was pushed away by a fierce determination that flooded the bond.

We must stop it, Hikari said. *There is no one here strong enough but us.*

Kai wasn't so sure about that, but the dragon's confidence bolstered her spirit. She nodded and climbed back onto the dragon's back. A horn blared behind her, and Kai looked over her shoulder to see the Sworn gathering into a formation.

They're going to try to attack it, Kai said.

Then we need to strike first.

Hikari leaped into the air and sailed over the army of Drakka, flying directly toward the monstrous beast. As they drew nearer, Kai pulled the Heart of Flame out of her bag and gripped it tightly. It pulsed in her hand, radiating a warmth that spread through her arm and into her chest.

The creature locked its fiery red eyes on them as they approached, seeming to recognize the threat they posed. It reared back, spreading its enormous wings, and roared again as it took to the air. The sound crashed over Kai, thick and heavy, like the weight of death itself. Hikari flinched, and Kai could feel a ripple of uncertainty in their bond.

Hikari banked to the side, dodging a sudden burst of dark liquid the creature spewed from its maw. It struck the ground below, burning through the Drakka horde and stone alike, leaving the ground scorched and sizzling.

In response, Hikari breathed her fire, sending a stream of flames hurtling toward the beast. The blaze met its dark scales, but to Kai's horror, they barely left a mark, flickering out as if snuffed by an invisible wind. Hikari whipped around to avoid a retaliatory swipe of its talons, and Kai's stomach lurched.

This creature was no ordinary dragon; it was something darker, something twisted by magic. They couldn't simply burn it—they needed a strategy.

We need to lead it away from the city, Kai said. *It'll give us time to find a weakness.*

Hikari rumbled in agreement and flew south, baiting the beast to follow. With a furious roar, it trailed after them like a shadow of death. It quickly gained on them with a speed that belied its size. Hikari angled upward, climbing higher into the sky. The beast continued to follow them, and Kai spotted a faint glow on its chest, a purple, pulsating light that reminded her of a heartbeat.

I have an idea, Kai said.

CHAPTER SEVEN

They rose higher and higher, the clouds swirling in their wake. Kai watched the ground below shrink away. The air grew cold, biting at her face, and she shivered, her breath coming out in puffs.

Are you ready? Hikari asked.

Kai gripped the hilt of her sword, bracing herself.

Yes.

With a powerful thrust of her wings, the dragon soared into a patch of clouds. When she was certain the creature lost sight of them, Kai let go of Hikari. The wind whipped around her, screaming in her ears, and her cloak billowed out, fluttering like a shadow cast against the sky. She felt the fabric pulse with its strange magic, and she slipped into the shadow realm. Light bent and faded as she vanished, phasing into a world of shifting darkness.

She was still falling, but it was like falling through ink rather than air. The creature drew closer, and once it was within reach, Kai flickered back into the physical realm, reappearing just above the dragon's head, her sword raised high. Its eyes flared in shock at her sudden appearance, but it didn't have time to react.

Kai issued a fierce cry as she fell, driving her blade deep into the dragon's chest. It struck the pulsing purple light, and dark ichor spurted out, followed by a shockwave of energy. It erupted from the beast, burning her skin. She ignored the pain and pushed the sword deeper, locking eyes with the creature as it twisted its head to look down at her. For a brief moment, it stared back at her, something tortured and lost in its gaze.

With a guttural roar, the dragon flailed, its wings beating erratically as it plummeted toward the earth. Kai held her grip, willing every ounce of strength into her arms, and twisted the blade. The beast gave a gasp, its roar choked into silence as the darkness within it stilled. She jerked her blade free and kicked off from the beast just as Hikari swooped below, and she landed roughly on the dragon's back.

Well done, Hikari said. *But next time, perhaps something a little less dramatic.*

Kai couldn't help but smile at Hikari's teasing. They turned back toward the city, and Kai could see the Drakka were about to breach the walls. The Sworn and their dragons were trying to hold them off, but the horde of creatures was unending and their line of defense was riddled with gaps where soldiers had fallen.

Get me as close to the Drakka as you can.

Another plan? Hikari asked.

Yes, but less dramatic than the last one.

Hikari descended until she was gliding only a few feet above where the Drakka were gathered outside the walls. Kai tapped into the power of the Heart of Flame and directed it toward the ground, creating a fiery barrier. The heat seared the Drakka, forcing them to retreat. It was only a temporary reprieve, but it gave the Sworn time to clear the walls and regroup. Hikari landed behind the barrier as it began to fade.

There are so many, Kai said, staring at the legions of Drakka.

Hikari issued a wave of fire from her jaws, incinerating the enemies nearest to them.

It's not enough. We need to do more.

I'm open to suggestions, Hikari rumbled.

Kai could feel the elders of the past guiding her. She closed her eyes and took a deep breath, channeling the energy from the Heart. Simultaneously, she drew the shadows from the cloak, weaving the two together.

Release your flames again.

Hikari breathed her fire, bolstered by the Heart, and Kai released a surge of shadow energy. The two forces collided mid-air, intertwining in a mesmerizing dance of light and darkness.

The resulting blast was cataclysmic. A wave of searing heat and inky blackness swept across the battlefield, engulfing a vast swath of the Drakka forces. Their agonized screams were cut short as the devastating attack consumed them.

As the smoke cleared, Kai heard gasps and murmurs of awe from the Sworn on the walls. She caught sight of Jiro, his eyes wide with disbelief. Kai allowed herself a small smile, though her heart pounded with the effort of the attack.

The effect on the Drakka was immediate and profound. Their orderly ranks dissolved into chaos as the survivors scrambled to regroup. Kai watched with grim satisfaction as entire battalions turned tail and fled, their will to fight shattered.

"They're withdrawing," someone shouted.

The Drakka forces were in full retreat, their numbers dwindling with each passing moment. The Sworn, emboldened by this turn of events, pressed their advantage, driving the enemy further from the city walls. Victory was within reach, but Kai felt deep sorrow. So much life had been lost, both Drakka and man, and she knew the cost of this battle would be felt for generations to come.

The adrenaline that had fueled her throughout the battle was fading, leaving behind a bone-deep exhaustion that threatened to overwhelm her. Kai slumped forward against Hikari, her muscles screaming.

You need rest, Hikari said.

We're not done yet. If we let our guard down... she trailed off, too tired to finish the thought.

You've pushed yourself to your limit, the dragon replied, concern in her tone. *Rest, if only for a moment.*

"Kai?"

She turned to see Jiro and Ichiro. They had joined her on the battlefield, and their dragons regarded Hikari curiously.

"That was incredible," Ichiro said excitedly.

Jiro regarded his brother with raised eyebrows. "I would call it terrifying."

Kai smiled until she realized Jiro was serious.

"I thought we were about to lose the wall," Ichiro continued, "but you and your dragon turned the tide!"

Kai straightened, fighting against her fatigue. "Each of us played a part in this victory," she said softly.

"True, but you two made the difference. The way you wielded magic, how you and your dragon move as one... it was like watching a legend come to life."

Kai felt a warmth in her chest that had nothing to do with the Heart of Flame's power.

"You look pale," Jiro said. "You should probably get some rest."

With one last look at the battlefield, Kai nodded.

CHAPTER EIGHT

Dawn found Kai standing motionless atop the wall, surveying the charred landscape. The smell of smoke still hung in the air, and she wrinkled her nose. Her armor, once gleaming, now bore the scars of battle. Her blade, however, remained sharp and as dark as when she'd first received it.

Master Satoshi joined her, his expression solemn. "You fought well last night."

Kai inclined her head. "Thank you, Master. I only wish I could have done more."

A commotion at the edge of the battlefield drew their attention. A lone rider approached at a breakneck speed, his horse's flanks lathered with sweat.

"A messenger," Master Satoshi murmured, his brows furrowing.

Kai glanced at the other Sworn who had gathered nearby, noting the tightening of jaws and the subtle shifting of stances. They, too, had sensed their hard-won triumph might be short-lived. The gates were opened for the rider, and Kai followed Master Satoshi down to the courtyard, her heart thundering. Had the emperor heard about her bond with Hikari?

The messenger's voice trembled as he delivered the news, each word landing like the blow of a hammer. "Zhencheng is under siege. A massive force of Drakka have descended without warning. The city's defenses are overwhelmed."

A collective gasp rippled through those standing within earshot. Kai's blood turned cold, her mind reeling at the implications. Zhencheng was the heart of the empire.

"How is this possible?" Master Satoshi asked, more to himself than the messenger. His face lit up with realization. "The attack here was a ruse."

"A ruse? Why would the Drakka send such a large force here for a ruse?" Kai asked.

"To divert our attention from their true target."

Akuhara's words came back to her. *The empire will crumble, and in its place will be something new, something better.*

"She seeks to kill the emperor," Kai said.

"It would seem so," Master Satoshi replied. "And we cannot allow that."

He immediately began issuing orders, and soon, Kai was standing alone. The power she shared with Hikari could save Zhencheng, and the emperor, but using it risked exposing her secret. Master Satoshi had been clear the emperor would kill her for breaking the law. Was saving the innocent worth the consequences?

Kai thought so. Hikari did, too, based on the approval she felt flowing through their bond. She made her way to the stable, where her fellow Sworn were already at work preparing to leave. The air held a nervous energy as dragons snorted and shifted, sensing the urgency.

"Can you hand me that salve?" Siran asked, pointing to one of the jars that lined a series of shelves behind her. Kai obliged, and Siran applied the ointment to a gash on her dragon's flank.

"How is he faring?"

"He is strong, but this battle has taken its toll. I fear what we'll face in Zhencheng, especially without much rest."

Around them, the Sworn worked with efficiency. Armor was donned, supplies were packed, and weapons were gathered. Yet beneath the bustle, Kai sensed an undercurrent of fear—not just for themselves, but for the fate of the empire.

"Do you think we'll make it in time?" Ichiro asked, his usually jovial face etched with worry as he tightened his dragon's saddle.

Kai met his gaze, forcing a smile. "We have to try." She turned away from them, seeking a moment of solitude amidst the frantic preparations. She went to the stall where Hikari rested, her golden scales shimmering under the daylight that filtered in from the skylight overhead. The dragon lifted her head, her eyes meeting Kai's.

I am afraid, Kai admitted, sinking to the ground beside Hikari.

Afraid of what?

That I cannot defeat her.

The dragon rumbled softly in response, a wave of warmth and reassurance passing through the bond.

We will defeat her together, Hikari said. *We have overcome many challenges, and we will prevail over Akuhara as well. You are stronger than you know, and your heart is true.*

Kai drew strength from her words, and she nodded wordlessly. She reflected on the path that had brought her to this moment. Everything she had faced shaped her into who she was. Hikari was right, she was stronger than she realized. Master Satoshi's commanding voice cut through the air, drawing the Sworn to attention.

"Gather around," he said.

Kai joined the others, forming a tight circle around their leader.

"We fly into the heart of chaos against an enemy that outnumbers us." He paused, letting the gravity of his words sink in. "Our mission is to help the imperial army defend Zhencheng. If we cannot drive the Drakka back, then we must evacuate the emperor to safety."

Kai's mind conjured images of the capital under siege, nobles and commoners alike lying dead in the streets.

"Master," Jiro spoke up, bringing her back to the present. "How can we hope to succeed? Even if we get the emperor to safety, how long will that last before the Drakka come for him again? They will not give up the chase."

Master Satoshi's gaze hardened. "We are Sworn. Our strength lies not in our numbers, but in our unity, our determination. We will stand as one against this tide of darkness, and I have faith that we will rise above it."

A murmur of agreement rippled around the circle.

"We will need every Sworn and dragon at our disposal, which forces me to make an odd request. A few of us fell in battle last night, and although their dragons are grieving, we need soldiers who can command their power effectively. I trust each of you, and therefore I am relying on you to give me options. Who do you think is up to the task?"

Kai cleared her throat. "I know a few people."

CHAPTER NINE

The Sworn formation cut through the sky like an arrow, speeding toward Zhencheng. The landscape stretched below them, a breathtaking display of countless hues blending together like a woven rug. Mountains loomed, their peaks disappearing into the clouds, and valleys cradled rivers that flowed like snakes across the land. Kai's heart swelled as she gazed upon the beauty of her homeland.

The wind whipped at her hair and tugged at her clothes, but it didn't bother her. She closed her eyes and stretched her arms out, relishing the freedom she felt. There were no worries in the sky, no fears or doubts plaguing her mind. There was only the rush of the wind and the beat of Hikari's wings.

They flew for most of the morning, and when the sun reached its zenith, Master Satoshi directed them to land. The group descended on the outskirts of a dense wooded area, and Kai dismounted, stretching her legs.

"Take some time to eat and rest," Master Satoshi said. "We'll continue shortly."

Kai thought it was odd he didn't order anyone to keep watch, but she decided the Drakka would be foolish to try to ambush them without a large force. She hadn't seen any sign of them from the sky, and she assumed that was because they were focused on the assault of the capital. Ryn approached her and bowed his head in respect.

"I am indebted to you again," he said.

"I didn't think you would agree," Kai replied. "Given your feelings for the empire, I mean."

Ryn looked past her to the trees and shrugged. "I would give anything to have my dragon back. This is the closest I'll ever get to that, so it was hard to decline."

"I understand. And the others?" She nodded toward the other Sundered, who kept themselves separated from the Sworn.

"They are of the same mind. We have been on our own for many years, and it is not easy being back among those whose loyalty lies with the empire. But we do not follow them. We follow you."

"I know you think it so, but I am not the Blooded One," Kai said softly.

"You may not carry the title, but you carry the spirit. You inspire hope where there is none, and your power is greater than any rider I have seen before. That is enough for me."

Kai was humbled by his words. Before she could respond, Ryn's eyes widened.

"Drakka!"

Kai whirled around and drew her sword, her eyes scanning the trees. "Where? I don't see anything."

"They are on the move. We need to stop them before they alert others."

Kai sprinted into the woods, weaving between the trees. She didn't need to go far before she spotted dark shapes moving through the underbrush. Following them, she burst through a bush, coming face to face with a Drakka scout. Without hesitation, she swung her blade. The Drakka blocked her strike and snarled, its eyes filled with malice.

Slipping into the shadows with the power of her cloak, Kai faded from view and reappeared behind the confused creature, thrusting her blade into its back. It gurgled and dropped to its knees. Placing her foot along its spine, Kai ripped her sword free and the Drakka fell face-first onto the ground. Siran and Jiro stood a few feet away, staring at her.

"Why are you just standing there? There are more of them. Hurry!"

Kai ran in the direction the other Drakka had fled in, and Siran and Jiro caught up to her. The three of them trailed after the Drakka, their steps thudding against the forest floor. Branches whipped at their faces and arms, but they pushed through the stinging pain, determined to catch the scouts before they alerted a larger force.

They chased the Drakka deeper into the woods, the undergrowth becoming denser as they went. The creatures moved swiftly, but they were hindered by the thick brush. As they rounded a bend, Kai skidded to a stop, holding out an arm to halt Siran and Jiro behind her. Through the trees, she could see a small clearing where a group of Drakka had gathered, their dark green scales blending with the colors of the forest. They appeared to be in the midst of a heated discussion, their snarls and hisses filling the air.

Kai crouched low, signaling for her companions to do the same. She knew they couldn't take on a group of Drakka this size on their own. They needed a plan.

Where are you? Kai asked Hikari.

I'm flying over the trees, but I can't see anything through the canopy. What's happening?

Kai sent an image of what she saw to the dragon, but Hikari only flooded the bond with her confusion. A twig snapped behind them, and the Drakka turned toward them. Kai jerked her head around to see Ichiro. He nodded at her before a whistling sound filled the air, and an arrow struck him in the chest. He staggered back from the force and collapsed to the ground.

"Ichiro!" Jiro rushed to his brother's side.

The sound of battle filled the air, and Kai turned back to the clearing to see Ryn and the other Sundered fighting the Drakka. Siran charged into the clearing, sword flashing as she joined the fray.

Kai scrambled over to Ichiro. The arrow had struck perfectly within a gap in his armor. Blood was welling from the wound, and Kai pressed her hand against it to staunch the flow. Ichiro groaned in pain, and Jiro cradled his brother's head in his lap.

"Stay awake," he urged.

"We have to get him out of here. Master Satoshi will know what to do. Can you help me carry him?"

Jiro nodded and rose to his feet. Kai grabbed onto his legs and Jiro grabbed his arms, and together they carried him out of the woods. The camp was on high alert, and the Sworn were stationed on all sides, weapons drawn and ready.

Master Satoshi saw them as they exited the trees, and he called for a physician. Kai and Jiro set Ichiro down gently, and the physician took over, examining the wound. Without explaining anything, Kai sprinted back into the woods, heading for the clearing. When she returned, the Drakka were using their power over the earth, summoning tree roots from the ground to attack the Sundered.

Ryn and his men had exhausted their strength and were beginning to lose ground. Kai used her cloak to fade into the shadow realm, moving through the trees like a ghost and slaying one Drakka after another. The Sundered renewed their attack, and soon the entire group of creatures were dead.

"Is that all of them?" Kai asked after returning to the physical world.

Ryn tilted his head to the side as if he were listening to something, then nodded. "I don't sense any others. I think we killed them all."

Kai wiped her sword on one of the bodies and sheathed it. "Good. Did anyone suffer an injury?"

"No. We were lucky."

"Luck had nothing to do with it, I'm sure," she replied, smiling. "You are all skilled warriors."

Ryn bowed his head to her. They walked together through the woods, and when they returned to the camp, many of the Sworn gave Kai curious stares. She approached Master Satoshi.

"How is Ichiro?" she asked.

"He will survive, though he will not be able to fight. His dragon is going to take him back to Dangju."

Relief washed over Kai. "That is great news. Why is... everyone staring at me?"

"Word of your deeds in the woods is spreading."

"They're afraid of me now, aren't they?"

"Fear often stems from a lack of understanding," Master Satoshi said, placing a comforting hand on her shoulder. "Your secret is safe, do not worry about that. I will ensure they know you are no different than any other Sworn."

"Thank you, Master," she whispered.

"Eat something and prepare yourself. We need to press on."

The journey resumed, and they flew until night, making camp on a plateau among the mountains. Kai's exhaustion led to the first full night of rest she had experienced in days. Just before dawn broke, Master Satoshi roused them all, offering them steamed rice for breakfast before ordering them back on the move.

They flew for several hours, and as Zhencheng came into view on the horizon, a sudden gust of wind buffeted them, causing the dragons to sway precariously. Kai's grip on Hikari tightened as she squinted ahead.

Something isn't right, she told her dragon. *This isn't natural.*

No sooner had the words left her mind than a wall of swirling clouds materialized before them, crackling with purple lightning. The storm appeared out of nowhere, its intensity reminding Kai of the storm that had battered Ikje before the Ceremony of Oaths.

Drakka magic, Hikari said. *I can sense it.*

Kai knew they couldn't turn back, not when they were so close. Drawing upon their bond, she reached out with her senses, probing the magical storm.

I think I can guide us through it, she said. *Take us up to Master Satoshi.*

The dragon sped up, taking them to the lead position.

"Let me take the lead!" she shouted, trying to be heard above the wind. "Tell them to follow me!"

Master Satoshi nodded, waving them onward. Hikari took point, and the Sworn fell into position behind them. Kai closed her eyes, focusing on the ebb and flow of the magical energies surrounding them. *Can you sense it?* she asked the dragon.

Yes. The path is treacherous, but not impassable.

With a deep breath, Kai opened her eyes and urged Hikari forward, diving into the heart of the storm. Lightning crackled around them, the wind threatening to tear them from the sky. But Kai remained focused, guiding the group through the maelstrom with a combination of instinct and her magical abilities.

Left! she said, and Hikari banked sharply, narrowly avoiding a tendril of purple lightning. *Now up!*

For what felt like an eternity, they navigated the magical tempest until, finally, with a last burst of speed, they emerged on the other side, the storm dissipating behind them. Cheers erupted from the Sworn as they realized they'd made it through the storm. Master Satoshi retook the lead. He glanced at her, his lips curled into a small, satisfied smile. There was something deeply personal about it, as though the pride bloomed not for anyone else's eyes but her own.

Kai nodded at him in return, her chest tight with a mix of exhilaration and unease. She knew her powers were growing, but at what cost?

The landscape below grew desolate. Scorched earth and abandoned villages told the tale of the Drakka's advance. Kai's mood grew somber. The once-verdant lands surrounding the capital were now a wasteland, and in the distance, she could see the faint glow of fires.

How many innocents have suffered already? she wondered.

Hikari's reassuring presence filled her mind. *We will avenge them.*

In the distance, the imposing walls of Zhencheng finally came into view, but instead of being a beacon of hope, they now stood as a last bastion against the encroaching darkness. The Drakka horde's presence was unmistakable, their war machines and dark magic a plague on the land. Kai swallowed hard, steeling herself for the battle to come.

If we fall... she trailed off.

If we fall, we will do so in a blaze of glory, Hikari said.

CHAPTER TEN

The great city of Zhencheng stood before Akuhara like a stubborn ember refusing to be snuffed out. Its high walls bristled with imperial soldiers, and Sworn flew overhead. Even from the ridge where she stood, she could see the banners of the emperor flapping defiantly in the wind, their golden threads shimmering in the light.

Her forces gathered below, a seething mass of Drakka that filled the air with their snarls and growls. She had summoned every last one of them, from the smallest hatchlings to the mightiest warriors. This was to be her final strike, the crushing blow that would end the empire once and for all. And yet, her fists clenched with rage.

Dangju. The name burned in her mind like a brand. When the news of the Drakka's defeat there had reached her, she had screamed out in anger and frustration. A city that should have been reduced to ash now still stood, thanks to the intervention of her sister.

Kai.

Akuhara turned sharply, seething with fury as she strode into her tent. The space was illuminated with a brazier that burned brightly, the glow casting shadows across the maps and battle plans sprawled on the table. Her dragon followed, sticking his head through the tent flaps, its molten eyes gleaming with curiosity and concern.

You let your rage consume you, it said, its voice a low rumble.

Be silent, Akuhara snapped, slamming her hands onto the table. Her breath came in short, furious bursts as she stared at the map of Zhencheng. Her claws of dark magic traced the city's defenses, searching for weaknesses, for any crack she could exploit.

She's here, Akuhara said finally, her voice trembling with a mix of anger and something she didn't want to admit. Fear. *Kai has brought more Sworn to defend the city. She's grown stronger. Too strong.*

The dragon stretched closer, its massive head close enough that she could feel his breath. *You have faced her before. You can face her again. And this time, you will defeat her.*

Akuhara shook her head, her hands balling into fists. *She's different now. Every time, she becomes more than what I expect. More than what I can overcome. She has an elder dragon, and now she has the Heart of Flame and that cloak. How am I supposed to stop that?*

The dragon's molten eyes narrowed. *You have an entire horde at your command. You have me. She is but one.*

"She is not just one!" Akuhara shouted aloud, slamming her fist against the table hard enough to crack the wood. She drew in a ragged breath, her shoulders trembling. *She is cut from the same cloth I am. And she will not stop until she has won.*

Silence hung in the air, thick and suffocating. Akuhara turned away, her gaze drifting to the back of the tent. Outside, the roars of the Drakka echoed through the encampment, their bloodlust palpable. She knew she could unleash them, let them overwhelm the city in a tide of fire and destruction. But it wouldn't just be the empire that fell. It would be everything. Possibly even her.

"I have to end this," Akuhara whispered, her voice barely audible. "No more retreats. No more waiting. Zhencheng must burn."

Her dragon rumbled in agreement, but there was a note of caution in its tone. *Then you must steel yourself. She will not show mercy. And neither can you.*

Akuhara straightened, her expression hardening into a mask of resolve. She left the tent, her mind churning with doubt and fear, but she buried it deep beneath the weight of her anger. If she was to face Kai again, it would be on her terms. And this time, she would not falter.

She magically projected her voice, her tone cold and unyielding.

"Attack!"

CHAPTER ELEVEN

The smell of smoke stung Kai's nostrils as they circled above the imperial city. War drums reverberated through the air, mingling with the guttural roars of the Drakka—a relentless tide that stretched as far as the horizon. Their hulking forms churned the earth into a foul mire, destroying everything underfoot.

Imperial soldiers stood atop the walls, their faces pale but their weapons steady. Archers loosed volleys of arrows, though many found no purchase on the Drakka's thick, armored hides. Siege engines hurled flaming pitch and vats of boiling oil were poured onto the attackers, but the sheer mass of the enemy was undiminished. For every Drakka that fell, a dozen more surged forward, climbing over the corpses of their own kind in their insatiable hunger to breach the city.

And somewhere out there, Kai knew, was her sister. She viewed it all with a grim expression, hope slowly giving way to despair.

How can we hope to turn back such a tide? she asked.

We have no other choice but to succeed, Hikari replied.

Master Satoshi returned from speaking with the emperor, his dragon flying to the center of their formation. He shouted to be heard above the noise, his voice cutting through the chaos.

"The emperor has given us one final order: we are to break through the Drakka lines and cut the head from the snake." As he spoke, he looked at Kai. "We must draw her out and defeat her by any means necessary."

Kai knew the true meaning behind his words: she was tasked with stopping Akuhara. She offered a silent nod of acceptance. They had battled once before, and while Kai had won, her sister's power was not to be underestimated.

Any ideas on how to find her? Hikari asked.

Kai scanned the Drakka's ranks, but there was no sign of Akuhara. *We need to do something to gain her attention.*

"I'll need the Sundered," Kai told Master Satoshi.

"Take whoever you need. The rest of us will do what we can to keep the Drakka away from the walls."

Kai motioned to Ryn, and Hikari descended from the sky, releasing a torrent of flame that carved a swath through the Drakka, incinerating dozens in a single breath. Behind her, the Sundered followed. Ryn led his men on a midnight-black dragon, striking like a shadowy harbinger of death. The Sundered flew in a tight formation, their blades flashing and magic crackling as they dove into the fray.

Kai clung to Hikari's saddle, her hair whipping in the wind as they dove toward a group of Drakka. With a wordless cry, she unleashed the Heart of Flame, the artifact flaring in her grasp. A fiery shockwave erupted, scattering the creatures like leaves in a storm. But the creatures were relentless, and Hikari wheeled upward as Drakka swarmed toward them, their talons raking the air.

Kai looked for her sister, but she was nowhere to be found. Her eyes narrowed as she saw a massive Drakka—a creature twice the size of its kin—charging toward the city's outer gate. Its flesh gleamed like obsidian, and a crown of twisted horns adorned its head.

I don't know what that is, but it can't be good, Kai said.

Should we try to stop it? Hikari asked.

Kai hesitated. *No. We need to find Akuhara.*

Hikari surged higher into the smoke-filled sky, her wings beating with powerful strokes as the sounds of battle below grew dimmer. Kai scanned the battlefield, but Akuhara was still nowhere to be seen.

We need a distraction big enough to draw Akuhara out. Something she can't ignore.

Before she could decide what that might be, she noticed the Drakka were swarming to one side of the walls. It wasn't chaos, it was coordinated, almost as if—

Her heart sank as she spotted it: a breach in the wall. Drakka were pouring through like water from a broken dam. "No," she whispered, her mind racing. They couldn't lose the city. Kai made a split-second decision.

Take me down there, she told Hikari, gripping the dragon tightly as they did a spiraling dive down toward the wall. They landed amidst the Drakka horde, and Hikari let out a deafening roar. The Drakka faltered for a moment, and Kai wasted no time in channeling the Heart of Flame, unleashing a wave of fire that consumed the nearest enemies in an inferno.

Hikari breathed her own flames, and with a primal growl, Kai thrust her hands forward, guiding the fire toward her dragon's flames. The two streams merged, growing, twisting, until a massive wall of searing heat erupted before them.

The Drakka's advance halted abruptly, their war cries turning to screams of confusion and pain. The barrier of fire stretched across the breach, an impenetrable curtain of flickering orange and gold. Kai's arms trembled with the effort of maintaining the spell. She was buying them time to seal the breach, but she knew it wouldn't be enough.

Her gaze swept across the walls, taking in the battered defenses, the exhausted soldiers, and the relentless enemy that still pressed against her fiery barrier. A sudden, bone-chilling roar echoed through the chaos.

Kai's heart skipped a beat as she turned to see the massive obsidian Drakka charging towards them, its horns gleaming in the firelight. The other Drakka in the vicinity seemed to part like a dark sea, making way for the formidable creature. Its eyes locked onto Kai, and a shiver ran down her spine. This Drakka was no ordinary beast; it exuded an aura of power and malevolence that made even Hikari falter for a moment.

Just as she felt her strength slipping, Ryn and the other Sundered joined the fray, attacking the enormous Drakka. Their dragons unleashed torrents of flame, lightning, and ice, their ferocity unmatched.

But it wasn't enough. The Drakka were too many, their ranks too deep. Even the Sundered's heroics couldn't tilt the balance for long. They needed a miracle.

CHAPTER TWELVE

"The breach is sealed!" Master Satoshi shouted.

It was a small victory, but it bolstered Kai's spirit nonetheless. She turned her attention back to the enormous Drakka. At the risk of breaking her concentration, she slipped off the dragon's back and stood beside her.

Help me take him down, Kai said to Hikari.

I'm ready when you are.

"Ryn!" Kai shouted. "Pull back!"

He did as she asked, and the other Sundered followed his command to do the same. With them out of the way, Kai turned the flames from the wall toward the Drakka, forcing the wall to enclose around the creature. The Drakka clawed at the barrier, its massive form silhouetted against the flames. Its roars of defiance turned to pained cries as the flames seared its flesh, but still, it pushed forward with unnatural strength. Kai gritted her teeth and focused all her energy on maintaining the spell, her body trembling with exertion.

With a thunderous roar, Hikari lunged forward through the wall of fire, crashing into the Drakka. Their clash sent shockwaves through the ground beneath Kai as they grappled for dominance. Kai released the magic and drew her sword, hesitating as her vision swam. It quickly cleared and she rushed ahead, swinging her blade in an arc that separated the Drakka's head from its shoulders. A cheer rose from the defenders on the walls.

But the fight wasn't over yet. More Drakka surged forward, their hatred fueled by the fall of their comrade. A host of Sworn and their dragons landed on either side of Kai, joining the battle. Kai climbed onto Hikari's back, and the Sworn shifted into an arrowhead formation. Kai felt Hikari's muscles tense beneath her, ready to lead the charge.

"Together!" Kai shouted.

"Together!" the others echoed in unison.

The air filled with the clash of battle as dragons and Drakka collided. Kai guided Hikari with subtle shifts of her weight, their minds working as one. They pressed into the Drakka'a ranks, striking quick, deadly blows, leaving destruction in their wake.

The tide of battle began to shift, slowly but inexorably. Kai watched with growing elation as the Drakka's lines started to fracture under the Sworn's relentless assault. Streams of fire, ice, and lightning arced through the sky as the Sworn unleashed their elemental powers in perfect harmony.

Kai felt a surge of pride and hope. Feeling bold, she experimented with the cloak's capabilities by extending its power to cover Hikari as well. She succeeded, but it took a toll on her. She used it in bursts, guiding Hikari through the shadow realm to appear where they were needed most, reappearing to offer support and direction.

"They're faltering!" Kai called out, her heart racing. "Keep pressing!"

As if in response to her words, the Drakka's formations began to crumble. Their fearsome roars turned to shrieks of frustration and pain as they found themselves outmaneuvered at every turn. A horn blasted through the air, and the Drakka began to retreat.

Akuhara is close, Kai said. *Take me up.*

Hikari took to the air, and Kai scanned the ground. There was still no sign of her sister. She watched the waves of Drakka pull back from the city, but she knew it was only a brief respite. As long as Akuhara was out there, the Drakka would not relent. They returned to the ground, and Master Satoshi was waiting among the Sworn.

"You have proven yourself a leader," he said to Kai. "The Sworn rallied to you on their own."

"I was only doing what any of us would do," Kai replied.

"We must rally our forces and prepare for the next wave. What we've seen is only the beginning."

Master Satoshi was right. The next wave of Drakka would arrive, and once again, the city's defenses would be tested to their limits. They needed rest, but there was no time to waste. Master Satoshi began issuing orders, organizing their forces and preparing for the impending onslaught.

It wasn't long before a scout arrived with the news that the Drakka had regrouped.

"How many?" Master Satoshi asked.

"More than before. Far more." The scout's voice quavered. "And the sky... it's not natural."

Dark storm clouds swirled on the horizon, tinged with an eerie green glow. A low rumble shook the ground, as if the earth itself trembled in fear. In the distance, a vast sea of shadows appeared on the horizon, stretching as far as the eye could see. The Drakka had returned.

As Kai watched, a figure rose above the ranks, terrible and familiar. Akuhara. Beside her loomed a monstrous shape—her dragon, wreathed in green light and flame. The air grew heavy, charged with an oppressive energy that made it hard to breathe. Kai felt a presence at her side and turned to see Siran, her face grave.

"By the ancestors," she breathed. "There are so many..."

The storm clouds roiled overhead, and in the distance, Akuhara's dragon let out a bone-chilling roar. Kai closed her eyes, reaching deep within herself for the strength she would need in the coming battle. The elements answered her call, fire and earth surging through her veins.

I am with you, Hikari said. *We will defeat her together.*

Master Satoshi's voice cut through the tension, drawing Kai from her thoughts. He stood atop a nearby battlement, his hair whipping in the wind as he addressed the gathered defenders.

"Sons and daughters of Zhencheng!" he bellowed. "The enemy stands at our gates, but they shall find no easy victory here! We are the guardians of this land, and our spirits burn brighter than their dark clouds! Remember those who came before us, who gave their lives so that we might stand here today! We are Sworn, and we will not falter!"

A chorus of cheers erupted from the defenders. Kai raised her fist in solidarity, her heart pounding with a mix of fear and determination. She ran a hand along Hikari's scales.

The dragon rumbled in response, a plume of smoke curling from her nostrils.

A deafening crash shook the foundations of the city. In the distance, massive boulders arced through the air, smashing against Zhencheng's outer walls.

"They've brought siege engines!" someone shouted.

Kai's mind raced. "Hikari, we need to—"

Before she could finish her sentence, another volley slammed into the defenses. The air filled with the screams of panicked civilians and the shouts of soldiers rushing to their posts.

"Multiple breaches!" came a frantic cry from beyond the wall. "They're attacking from all sides!"

CHAPTER THIRTEEN

The world blurred as Hikari took flight, her powerful wings carrying them above the chaos. From their vantage point, Kai's heart sank at the sight below. The outer walls had crumbled in several places, and streams of Drakka forces poured through the gaps like a toxic flood.

We can't let them reach the palace, Kai said.

Hikari growled in agreement, diving towards the nearest breach. Kai called forth gouts of flame to rain down upon the invaders. Screams of pain and rage echoed up from below. As they banked for another pass, Kai caught sight of terrified civilians fleeing through the streets.

We need to buy them time, she said, more to herself than to Hikari. *Head for the main gate!*

They soared over the city, Kai's stomach twisting at the destruction below. Fires raged unchecked, smoke billowing into the sky. The sound of clashing steel and agonized cries filled the air. Landing near the gate, Kai leapt from Hikari's back.

"Where is Master Satoshi?" she asked a nearby guard.

"He was summoned by the emperor."

Hold this position, she told Hikari.

Kai ran through the streets. The Drakka's assault was relentless, far beyond what she had imagined. She reached the palace and strode in without challenge as the guards were absent. As she burst into the imperial chambers, the scene before her made her blood run cold.

The emperor, his face ashen, was surrounded by cowering advisors. "We have no choice," he was saying, his aged voice trembling. "We must surrender before all is lost."

"Your Majesty!" Kai shouted, striding forward. All eyes turned to her, including Master Satoshi's who stood next to the emperor's throne. "You can't surrender."

The emperor's eyes narrowed. "Zhencheng is falling. To continue this fight is to doom our people to slaughter."

Kai shook her head vehemently. "I can stop this. I can face Akuhara directly."

Master Satoshi leaned in close and whispered into the emperor's ear. Kai couldn't help but wonder if he was betraying her. The emperor studied her for a long moment, conflict clear on his face. Finally, he nodded.

"I won't fail," she promised. "Keep the emperor safe," she added, looking at Master Satoshi. He nodded, and Kai left the palace, sprinting back toward the main gate of the city.

It's time to end this, she told Hikari as she slid to a halt beside the dragon. *I'll deal with Akuhara. You keep her beast busy.*

Hikari took flight with a loud roar, disappearing over the wall. Kai slipped through the gate, which had been pushed ajar by a large boulder. She scanned the battlefield and found Akuhara leading a group of Drakka, power crackling around her like a sinister aura. Kai tightened her grip on her hilt and rushed out to meet her.

"I should have known I'd find you here," her sister said. "You've become quite a thorn in my side."

"Allow me to ease your suffering."

Without warning, Akuhara struck. Dark tendrils of magic, intertwined with searing flames, lashed out towards Kai. She barely had time to react. She dove to the side, channeling her connection to the earth. The ground trembled, responding to her will. A wall of stone burst from the ground, shielding her from the worst of Akuhara's onslaught.

"You can't beat me," Akuhara taunted, unleashing another barrage of dark fire that melted the stone. "You're too weak, too afraid to seize true power!"

Gritting her teeth, Kai drew upon the Heart of Flame's magic, pushing her sister's flames aside. "You're wrong," she replied, her voice steady despite the strain. "Strength isn't about domination. It's about doing what's right, even when it costs you everything."

Akuhara's eyes flashed with malice as she summoned a whirlwind of shadows, her fingers twisting in arcane gestures. "Such noble sentiments won't save you or this empire. I told you before, I'm going to burn this world and create something new."

The dark tempest surged towards Kai, crackling with energy. Kai's instincts took over. She thrust her hands forward, calling upon the Heart of Flame. A brilliant wall of fire erupted before her, intertwining with wisps of shadow she conjured from the shadow realm.

"I won't let you destroy anything else!" Kai shouted.

Their powers clashed in a dazzling spectacle. Streams of fire and shadow danced around them, the air sizzling with energy. Kai drew upon the earth, causing the ground to shift and buckle beneath Akuhara's feet. Her sister stumbled but quickly regained her footing, retaliating with a torrent of water from the sky that threatened to drown Kai where she stood. Kai countered the magic by super-heating the air, turning the deluge to steam.

"Clever," Akuhara grudgingly admitted, her eyes narrowing. "But you are a novice compared to me."

Kai's breath came in short gasps. She could feel the strain of maintaining such intense elemental manipulation. But she couldn't falter now. With a swift motion, Kai summoned a gust of wind, using it to propel herself into the air. From this vantage point, she rained down a barrage of fireballs, each one aimed at pushing Akuhara back.

She couldn't keep this up much longer.

Kai felt the familiar warmth of Hikari's presence brush against her mind. In that moment of connection, a surge of strength flooded through her. She closed her eyes briefly, drawing a deep breath.

Show her your true power.

The words came from their bond, but it wasn't Hikari voice she heard. It was Kokoro's. With a fluid motion, Kai unfurled the dragon skin cloak, its scales shimmering with an otherworldly light. As she wrapped it around herself, she slipped into the shadow realm. The battlefield around her became muted, ghostly. She could see Akuhara, but her sister's movements were sluggish, as if she were moving through water.

Kai darted through the shadows, emerging behind Akuhara. She kicked the back of her leg, dropping her sister to her knees. Akuhara rose and whirled around, but Kai was already gone, melting back into the shadows. She reappeared at Akuhara's left, summoning a whirlwind of fire that caught her twin off guard.

"Stand still and fight me!" Akuhara roared.

Kai felt a pang of sadness. "I am fighting you," she said. "But on my terms, not yours!"

As she danced between realms, Kai could feel the tide of battle shifting. Akuhara's attacks, once so overwhelming, now seemed clumsy and predictable. With each pass, Kai used the elements—fire to blind, earth to trap, and air to buffet.

Akuhara's fury grew with each failed assault. "You think your parlor tricks can save you?" she screamed, unleashing a massive wave of dark energy.

But Kai was ready. She emerged from the shadows directly in front of her sister, her hands weaving an intricate pattern, guided by the elder dragons of the past. The elements responded to her call, forming a shimmering barrier that absorbed Akuhara's attack.

With a gesture, she turned Akuhara's own dark energy against her, sending it crashing back in a dazzling display. For the first time, Kai saw fear flicker in her sister's eyes. With a bone-chilling scream, Akuhara thrust her hands skyward. The air crackled as darkness swirled around her, coalescing into a maelstrom of pure destructive force.

Kai closed her eyes, placing a hand over the Heart of Flame. Its warmth pulsed in sync with her heartbeat, and she felt Hikari's strength flowing through her. With a deep breath, Kai channeled the Heart of Flame's power. Fire erupted from her hands, meeting Akuhara's assault head-on. The clash of energies lit up the battlefield, casting eerie shadows across the city's walls.

Kai gritted her teeth, her arms trembling with the effort. Slowly, inch by inch, Kai's fire began to push back against Akuhara's darkness. The air shimmered with heat, the ground beneath their feet splintering from the immense pressure.

The Heart of Flame blazed brighter than ever, its power coursing through Kai's veins. With tears streaming down her face, she gathered her strength for one final push, but as the flames engulfed Akuhara, her resolve wavered.

CHAPTER FOURTEEN

Despite everything, a flicker of hope burned within Kai. She extended her hand, her voice soft yet urgent.

"Abandon this path," she pleaded. "It doesn't have to end this way."

Akuhara's lips curled into a sneer, her voice dripping with venom. "You naive child. The darkness is all I have."

With a snarl, Akuhara lunged forward, dark energy crackling around her fingertips. Kai's instincts kicked in, her elemental powers surging forth. She thrust her hands outward, invisible forces pinning Akuhara to the ground.

Kai's heart pounded like a drum, refusing to slow. Was this truly the only way? But as she gazed into Akuhara's hate-filled eyes, she knew there was no other choice.

With a heavy heart, Kai unsheathed her black-bladed sword. The weight of it felt different now, as if it carried the burden of what she must do. She raised the blade high, its obsidian surface reflecting the chaos around them.

Akuhara struggled against her invisible tethers, but it was no use.

"I'm sorry," Kai whispered. Their eyes met, and Kai drove the sword deep into Akuhara's heart.

A terrible scream tore from Akuhara's throat, darkness exploding outward. Kai stumbled back, her eyes wide as she watched the light fade from her sister's gaze. Her dragon roared in pain and broke away from Hikari, flying awkwardly before crashing to the ground in a shower of dust. Hikari streaked through the sky, landing atop the fallen dragon and ending his thrashing.

As Akuhara's body went limp, a ripple of uncertainty passed through the Drakka forces. Kai could sense their faltering resolve, but knew the danger was far from over. Their leader had fallen, but they still threatened to overwhelm the city.

Kai closed her eyes, reaching deep within herself. She felt the warm pulse of her bond with Hikari, the fiery energy of the Heart of Flame, and the ancient power of the dragon-skin cloak on her shoulders. The elements swirled around her, responding to her call.

"No more," Kai declared, her voice carrying across the battlefield. She began to weave the disparate energies together, guided by ancient knowledge that funneled through the bond.

As the power built within her, Kai's thoughts turned to the weight of her duty. How many lives hung in the balance? How much would be sacrificed to secure peace? The questions burned in her mind as she channeled every ounce of her strength into her impending strike.

Her eyes snapped open, blazing with an otherworldly light. The combined power of the elements and shadows surged through her, burning brighter and fiercer than anything she'd felt before. It was as if every fiber of her being had become a conduit for pure, unbridled energy.

Hikari howled with anguish, the dragon's pain and determination echoing Kai's own. Their bond, already strong, deepened to an almost unbearable level. Kai could feel Hikari's heartbeat as if it were her own, their minds melding until she wasn't sure where she ended and the dragon began.

I don't know if I can contain this, Kai cried out to Hikari.

Your strength is mine, and mine is yours. Take what you need.

As the power continued to build, Kai felt a searing pain across her back. The cloak began to tear under the strain of the elemental forces coursing through it. With each rip, Kai felt her connection to the elements fracture, threatening to slip away entirely.

Despite the agony ripping through her body and the danger of losing control, Kai pressed on. She raised her hands, channeling every ounce of power she could muster. The very fabric of reality seemed to warp around her.

With a final, earth-shattering cry, Kai released the pent-up energy. A fiery explosion of magic erupted from her hands, engulfing the Drakka forces in a blinding inferno. The power was overwhelming, beautiful, and terrifying all at once.

As the magic poured out of her, Kai felt her consciousness begin to slip. Her thoughts turned to Hikari, of the unbreakable bond they shared, and she found comfort.

The deafening roar of the explosion faded, giving way to an eerie silence. As the smoke began to dissipate, Kai blinked, her vision blurry and unfocused. The bitter smell of ash and smoke filled her nostrils, making her cough weakly.

Hikari?

A low rumble answered her, and Kai felt the comforting presence of her dragon nearby. As her vision cleared, she saw the devastation that surrounded them. The army of Drakka lay in ruins, war machines crumbled and bodies torn asunder. She turned to Zhencheng and signs of life began to emerge.

Survivors, their faces streaked with soot and disbelief, cautiously peeked out from hiding places. A child's cry pierced the air, followed by the relieved sob of a mother. Slowly, people began to gather, their eyes fixed on Kai and Hikari with a mixture of awe and gratitude.

An elderly man approached, his robes tattered and covered in blood. "You... you saved us," he said, his voice trembling. "The Drakka... they're gone."

Kai tried to respond, but her strength was fading rapidly. The world began to spin, and she felt herself falling. *Hikari,* she reached out with her mind. *I can't...*

As consciousness slipped away, Kai felt the warm embrace of Hikari's wing enveloping her. The dragon's presence in her mind was a soothing balm, even as pain wracked both their bodies.

Rest, Hikar's voice echoed in her thoughts. *You have done more than enough. Zhencheng is safe.*

Kai's last coherent thought was of the immense toll their victory had taken. As darkness claimed her, she wondered if the price of peace would ever truly be paid in full.

CHAPTER FIFTEEN

As consciousness slowly returned, Kai's fingers instinctively sought the familiar texture of her cloak. Instead, they met tattered remnants, the once-powerful garment now reduced to frayed edges and gaping holes. She forced her eyes open, wincing at the effort.

"The cloak," she whispered, her voice hoarse. "It's..."

Hikari's rumbling voice filled her mind. *A casualty of our victory.*

Kai struggled to sit up, her body protesting every movement. She held the ruined cloak before her, its magical essence was gone, dissipated like mist in the morning sun. As she grappled with the loss, she felt her connection to the elements dim, like a candle guttering in the wind.

I can feel it, Kai said, a lump forming in her throat. *The elements... they're slipping away.*

Kai reached out with her senses. The earth beneath her felt muted, the air less responsive to her call. It was as if a part of herself had been torn away, leaving a hollow ache in its wake.

Was it worth it? she asked.

The dragon's eyes met hers, filled with a mixture of sorrow and pride. *Look around you. The city stands. Its people live. What is the price of a cloak compared to that?*

Kai nodded slowly, her fingers tracing the remnants of the magical garment. *You're right, of course. It's just...*

Her words were cut short by the sound of trumpets. The makeshift curtain of her recovery tent was drawn back, revealing an imperial messenger in resplendent, if slightly singed, robes.

"Kai Lin," the messenger announced, bowing deeply. "His Imperial Majesty requests your presence for a ceremony of honor. You and your dragon are to be celebrated as the saviors of Zhencheng."

Kai exchanged a glance with Hikari. *I'm not sure I'm in any condition for a ceremony,* she admitted.

The dragon's amusement rippled through their bond.

How long have I been unconscious?

A few days, Hikari replied. *They've been checking on you every hour to see if you've woken. They're desperate to pay honor to you.*

Kai wasn't sure how she felt about that, but she gingerly rose from her bed anyway. She made herself as presentable as possible and glanced around the tent curiously.

I wouldn't let them move you out of my sight, Hikari said, reading her thoughts. *They set this up where you collapsed.*

Kai laughed and immediately regretted it as pain flashed through her body. She winced, waiting for it to pass before stepping out of the tent. She followed the messenger, and Hikari stayed close behind her.

They entered what remained of the imperial palace, and Kai was surprised to see a large crowd filtering in for the ceremony. The throne room's ceiling was open to the sky, its roof nothing more than a memory. Her parents were there, and tears filled her eyes. With all of the chaos, she hadn't thought to ask Master Satoshi about them.

The emperor rose from his throne and stepped forward. "Kai Lin," he intoned, his voice carrying to every corner of the room. "You have done what many thought impossible. You have saved not just this city, but the very heart of our empire."

Kai bowed her head, feeling the weight of every gaze upon her. "Your Majesty, I—"

"No," the emperor interrupted, a smile gracing his features. "Today, it is we who bow to you." To Kai's astonishment, the emperor lowered himself to his knees, then pressed his head down to the ground at her feet in a gesture of deep respect.

As he straightened, the emperor's eyes gleamed with pride. "Kai Lin, your bravery and leadership have proven invaluable. I would have you stand among my council, to help guide our empire into this new era of peace."

A murmur of approval rippled through the crowd. Kai felt her heart racing, torn between duty and the nagging feeling that her path lay elsewhere. She glanced at Hikari, seeking guidance in her eyes.

"Your Majesty," Kai began, her voice steady despite her inner turmoil. "I am deeply honored by your offer..." She took a deep breath, feeling the weight of her decision. "...but I must respectfully decline." A collective gasp rippled through the crowd, and even the emperor's eyebrows raised in surprise.

"My path," Kai continued, her voice growing stronger, "lies not in the halls of power, but among the people I've sworn to protect. The war may be over, but the scars it left run deep. I wish to help rebuild what has been lost, to ensure that the lessons of this conflict are not forgotten. The threat of the Drakka isn't gone, not fully. There are nests out there that must be found and destroyed. These things are my path. With all due respect, I do not wish to be a figurehead on your council."

She met the emperor's gaze. "Your Majesty, you have the power to lead our people into a new era of peace and unity without me."

The emperor nodded slowly, a look of understanding dawning on his face. "Your wisdom continues to impress me, Kai Lin. Very well, I shall honor your decision."

Food was brought out from the royal kitchen, and Kai sat with her parents as they ate together. They spoke little, choosing instead to enjoy their time together. As the ceremony concluded, Kai felt a mixture of relief and anticipation. She turned to Hikari, who had been a silent presence throughout.

Are you ready for another journey?

Hikari's rumble was answer enough. She bade her family goodbye, and set out from Zhencheng with Ryn and the Sundered, leaving behind the cheers and accolades for the open sky.

As they traveled, the landscape gradually transformed. The scorched earth gave way to tender shoots of grass, and the smell of smoke was replaced by the sweet scent of wildflowers. Kai marveled at nature's resilience, feeling a spark of hope with each sign of renewal.

In a small village, they paused to rest. Kai watched as villagers worked together to rebuild homes, their faces etched with determination rather than despair. A young girl approached, offering Kai and her companions a handful of freshly picked berries.

"For the dragon rider who saved us," the child said, her eyes wide with admiration.

Kai accepted the gift with a smile, her throat tight with emotion. "Thank you," she murmured, realizing that this—this moment of simple kindness—was why she had accepted this path.

As they continued their journey, Kai's thoughts drifted to the challenges that lay ahead. Once the nests were destroyed, she wanted to repair Tatenagawa. The temple's restoration would be no small task, but she knew it was necessary. It would stand as a beacon of hope, a reminder of what could be achieved when people stood united against darkness.

CHAPTER SIXTEEN

As the days turned to weeks, Ryn sensed less of the Drakka eggs. They had destroyed over a dozen nests, and now they stood outside the entrance of the last one. The cavern loomed ahead of them, its jagged mouth yawning open as though the earth itself had split apart to spill its dark secrets. Kai stood at the entrance, her hand resting on the hilt of her sword. The air was thick with a cloying, sulfuric smell that made her stomach churn. Hikari shifted beside her, her golden scales glinting faintly in the light filtering through the stormy sky.

Behind them, the Sundered waited in silence. Ryn stepped forward, his face grim. "This is the largest nest we've found so far," he said, his voice low. "As soon as we can destroy this one, the Drakka threat will end for good."

Kai nodded, her gaze fixed on the darkness ahead. "We are almost done," she said. Her voice was steady, but a flicker of unease danced at the edge of her thoughts. Each nest they had destroyed had exacted its toll—on their strength, and on their spirits. For some reason she could not explain, destroying the eggs became a weight upon her, upon them all, that they could not ignore. She suspected it was a curse of some kind, perhaps an enchantment left behind by Akuhara.

Hikari's rumbling voice broke through her thoughts. *The eggs will not resist, but the act itself will strain you. You must be ready.*

I am, Kai said, her grip tightening on her sword. "We've come too far to falter now." Those last words were aimed at Ryn as she glanced over her shoulder.

Ryn nodded, signaling the others. The Sundered fell into formation, their weapons drawn. They were fewer now than when she had first met them. Each loss weighed on Kai's heart, but she pushed the grief aside. There would be time to mourn when the last remnants of the Drakka were gone.

The group moved into the cavern, the darkness swallowing them whole. The walls were slick with moisture, and the air grew warmer with each step. The faint, rhythmic pulsing of the eggs echoed through the chamber, a sound that sent a shiver down Kai's spine.

The nest was vast, its floor littered with clusters of eggs. Their translucent shells pulsed faintly with an ominous light.

"Spread out," Kai ordered.

The Sundered moved into position. Hikari unleashed a controlled stream of fire, the flames washing over the eggs. The outer shells hissed and cracked under the heat, the light within them flickering like dying embers.

Kai stepped forward, her sword raised, and brought it down in a clean strike. The egg shattered, its contents spilling out in a viscous, dark liquid. She moved to the next, and the next, each strike a step closer to the end of this nightmare.

The Sundered followed her lead, driving their blades through the eggs with grim determination. Hikari stood watch, using her flames to burn more eggs as they worked in sections. The cavern echoed with the sound of shattering shells and the heavy breaths of the Sundered.

When the last egg had been destroyed, Kai lowered her sword, her chest heaving with exhaustion. She looked around the cavern, now silent and empty. The weight of what they had done pressed down on her, but she refused to let it crush her. This was necessary. This was the cost of freedom.

Ryn stepped beside her, his face pale. "It's done."

Kai nodded, her eyes lingering on the scorched remains of the nest. "We've destroyed them all."

***

The village of Taepo was a husk of its former self. What once had been a bustling town with vibrant markets and colorful banners was now little more than ash and rubble. The pungent smell of smoke lingered in the air, mingling with the salty tang of the nearby sea. Kai stood in the center of the square, her gaze sweeping over the scene of devastation. Families picked through the wreckage of their homes, searching for anything salvageable. Children clung to their parents, their wide eyes filled with fear and uncertainty.

Hikari shifted behind her, her massive form casting a long shadow over the square. The sight of the golden dragon seemed to bring a mix of emotions from the villagers. Some looked at her with awe and gratitude, others with fear. Kai couldn't blame them. For years, dragons had been a sign that Drakka were nearby.

"We need to start with shelter," Kai said, turning to Ryn who stood at her side. "The villagers won't make it through winter exposed like this."

Ryn nodded, his expression grim. "There's enough wood in the forest to build temporary homes. I'll organize the Sundered to help."

"Thank you."

Ryn gave a curt nod and moved off to gather the others. Kai turned her attention back to the villagers. Taking a deep breath, she stepped onto the remains of what had once been a fountain, raising her voice to address the crowd.

"People of Taepo," she began. "I know you've suffered. I know the scars of the Drakka's attack run deep. But you are not alone. We are here to help you rebuild—not just your homes, but your lives. Together, we will restore what was lost and make it stronger."

The villagers paused in their work, their eyes turning to her. For a moment, there was only silence, and then a man stepped forward, his face lined with age and grief. "And what of the dragon?" he asked, his voice trembling. "Why is it here?"

Kai glanced back at Hikari, who lowered her head slightly, their eyes meeting. She turned back to the man, her voice firm. "Hikari is here to help, just as I am. There is nothing to fear anymore. The Drakka are gone."

The man hesitated, then gave a slow nod. The tension in the air eased, and the villagers returned to their work. Kai stepped down from the fountain, letting out a quiet sigh.

Winning hearts was proving to be as difficult as winning battles.

By midday, the square was alive with activity. The Sundered worked alongside the villagers, chopping wood, clearing debris, and erecting the frames of new homes. Kai joined them, rolling up her sleeves to lift beams and hammer nails while Hikari used her massive claws to help clear away larger pieces of rubble. The sight of the dragon working alongside them seemed to soften some of the villagers' fear, though others still kept their eyes on their surroundings.

"This beam goes here," Ryn called out, directing a group of villagers as they hoisted a support beam into place. Kai moved to help stabilize it, her arms straining against the weight. Together, they secured it, and the frame of a new home began to take shape.

"It's coming together," Ryn said, wiping sweat from his brow.

Kai nodded, her gaze drifting to a group of children who watched from the edge of the square. One of them, a boy no older than eight, clutched a tattered stuffed dragon in his hands. He stared at Hikari with a mixture of fascination and fear.

Kai crouched down, beckoning the boy over. He hesitated but eventually took a tentative step forward. "What's your name?" she asked gently.

"Jin," he said, his voice barely above a whisper.

Kai smiled. "Jin, would you like to meet Hikari?"

The boy's eyes widened, and he clutched his toy tighter. "She won't hurt me?"

"No," Kai said firmly. "Hikari would never hurt someone she's sworn to protect."

She extended a hand, and after a moment, Jin took it. Together, they approached Hikari, who lowered her massive head to their level. Kai placed a hand on the dragon's snout, encouraging Jin to do the same. The boy wavered, then reached out, his small hand trembling as it touched the warm, golden scales.

Hikari rumbled softly, a sound that seemed to vibrate through the ground. Jin's face lit up with a smile, and he turned to show his stuffed dragon to Hikari. "See? You look like him!"

Kai chuckled, and for a moment, the weight on her shoulders felt a little lighter. These small moments of connection were what would help heal the wounds left by the war.

By nightfall, the village square had transformed. Several frames for new homes stood tall, and the villagers gathered around a large fire in the center of the square. Kai sat with the Sundered, her body aching from the day's work but her heart full. Hikari lay curled nearby, her scales reflecting the firelight.

Ryn handed Kai a bowl of stew, and she accepted it gratefully. "It's a start," he said, nodding toward the progress they'd made.

Kai nodded. "A start is all we need. The rest will follow."

As the villagers shared stories and laughter around the fire, Kai allowed herself a rare moment of peace. The battle against the Drakka had been won, but the battle to rebuild was only beginning. Still, she couldn't help but feel hope stir within her. They had survived. They were moving forward. And together, they would rise from the ashes.

CHAPTER SEVENTEEN

In the spring, Kai returned to the crumbling ruins of the Tatenagawa temple, her eyes tracing the skeletal remains of the once-majestic pillars and archways. Fragments of ornate tiles crunched beneath her feet as she walked, each step stirring her memories.

It's strange, Kai said. *To be back where it all began.*

In her mind's eye, she saw the faces of those who had fallen: Kokoro, Liu, and countless others. "I won't let your sacrifices be in vain," she vowed, her fists clenching at her sides.

She gazed upon the ruins with renewed hope. Where others might see only destruction, Kai envisioned soaring spires and open courtyards. She could almost hear the laughter of young dragon riders echoing through restored halls.

What do you think, Hikari? Kai asked, turning to the dragon. *Can you see it too?*

Hikari's eyes met Kai's, a low rumble emanating from her chest. The dragon's tail swished, sending a small cascade of rubble tumbling down a nearby mound.

Kai chuckled. *I'll take that as a yes.*

She approached Hikari, her hand instinctively reaching for the Heart of Flame that hung at her waist. The dormant artifact was warm to the touch, a gentle reminder of the power that had once coursed through it.

"We won," Kai whispered, her voice thick with emotion. She stroked Hikari's scales, feeling the strong pulse of their bond.

As the words left her lips, the first rays of dawn crept over the horizon, bathing the ruins in a soft, golden light. Kai and Hikari stood side by side, their silhouettes merging as they gazed at the brightening sky.

In that moment, Kai felt a profound sense of peace settle over her. The road ahead would be long and arduous, but with Hikari by her side and the lessons of their journey etched in her heart, she knew they could face the many challenges that lay ahead.

Are you ready for the real work to begin?

Hikari's answering roar echoed across the land, heralding the dawn of a new era.

THE END

About the Author

Richard Fierce is a fantasy author with a passion for storytelling that dates back to his childhood. He first ventured into publishing in 2007 and hasn't looked back since. His books are filled with dragons, adventure, and the kind of epic journeys that transport readers to new worlds.

In 2000, Richard was named Poet of the Year for his poem The Darkness, and his love for literature extends beyond just writing—he co-founded the Acworth Book Festival in Georgia to help bring authors and readers together. Though he originally worked in retail, he eventually transitioned to the tech industry, balancing his career with his writing.

Richard lives in Northwest Georgia with his family and a lively mix of pets, including four dogs (huskies!). He often jokes that his house feels like a zoo, but he wouldn't have it any other way.

His love for fantasy started in high school when he was gifted a copy of *Dragons of Spring Dawning* by Margaret Weis and Tracy Hickman—a book that sparked a lifelong love for dragons and epic quests.

Whether he's writing about dragon riders, lost civilizations, or ancient prophecies, Richard Fierce continues to craft stories that pull readers into unforgettable adventures.